MY LAST DAYS

a novel

by
lou rowan

chiasmus press
Portland

Chiasmus Press

www.chiasmuspress.com
press@chiasmusmedia.net

Acknowledgements: many chapters of this novel first appeared in *Prague Literary Review*, *Journal of Experimental Fiction*, and *Golden Handcuffs Review*. Thanks to Big Top Productions, Marfa, Texas, for a residency that helped with this work. Thanks to Robert Sullivan, whose writings about Greater New York are lively as their subject.

PRODUCED AND PRINTED IN THE UNITED STATES OF AMERICA
ISBN: 0-9785499-6-1

cover design: Kevin Potis
layout design: Matthew Warren

"I am in earnest. I will try."

—Moby Dick

"Senators and presidents have climbed so high with pain enough, not because they think the place specially agreeable, but as an apology for real worth, and to vindicate their manhood in our eyes. This conspicuous chair is their compensation to themselves for being of a poor, cold, hard nature. They must do what they can. Like one class of forest animals, they have nothing but a prehensile tail: climb they must, or crawl."

—Ralph Waldo Emerson

To William Gaddis and Douglas Woolf
"Veritas"

MY LAST DAYS

Contents

1. CHERRY GETS ME GOING **7**
2. LESSONS FROM MY YOUTH **19**
3. A BLOW **31**
4. WORLD HISTORY **41**
5. THE PLOT **55**
6. WRESTLEMANIUS INTERRUPTUS **71**
7. DEVELOPING BEDFORD-STUYVESANT FOR THE FUTURE **79**
8. MY NEW SIDEKICK **87**
9. BIG BUSINESS BY THE YACHT **95**
10. DEATH **103**
11. ROUNDUP **107**
12. UP AND AWAY **113**

AFTERWORD: METROPOLIS *by* Toby Olson 117
winner PEN Faulkner Fiction Award

Illustrations by Quentin Rowan

1 CHERRY GETS ME GOING

Mom knew that excessive humility is pride in disguise. She taught me to show my best face and figure to the world—defining clear bounds of decency and hygiene. When I accepted my mission to the Metropolis, she designed the uniform that symbolizes my legend.

First we experimented with peel-on masks we ordered c.o.d. from Hollywood. Mom's original notion was to turn me bald, so that my blue-black hair wouldn't be disturbed by flight or by lightning-fast action: I'd be The Human Bullet, or The Man-Missile. (She harbored a crush on Yul Brynner at the time, the harmless straying that she and Dad never begrudged each other.) But the ventilation technology preventing overheating inside a mask awaited invention, and my instincts recoiled from hiding my good looks and changing the name I longed for.

"Clarkie, you have a right to be yourself," she declared, her warm heart sensing and loving my feelings. In these shining moments of blissful family inspiration, we decided that I should display my God-given potency whenever I was fulfilling my mission, but when I walked among ordinary mortals as one of them, I would be in disguise.

This policy determined, we hugged again, and we pondered my aerodynamics and my image with Dad, poring through my piles of *Popular Mechanics* and the *Life Magazines* on her coffee table for inspiration.

"I've got it, boys!"

She showed us a picture of Dame Margot Fonteyn leaping over the flaming fountain at the Hollywood Bowl. She chuckled at Dad's shaking head and my drooping shoulders, "It's o.k. boys. I know what I'm doing! You'll see. I'm going to cover you in glory, son. Shoo-shoo away."

Two hours later: "Here, Clarkie, try this. You'll have to watch your diet wearing this, sonny."

Thrilled by the fresh scent of the deep blue cotton leotard she'd cut and sewn, I rushed upstairs to my mirror, heart pounding harder than I ever remember. No team or scout uniform could prepare me for this ecstasy—I cannot imagine any American boy knowing what I knew then, my one truly liberating experience on earth beyond my calling from Dr. Pill. There I was—red, white and blue, plus a field of gold emblazoning the symbolic S over my heart. What an artist my Mom was: she combined the white of my skin with the blue leotard and the red S symbol to give me the motivation and inspiration of Old Glory. She bathed my S on a corn-yellow field to fill my heart with the kindness of Kansas. I explicate her work for you now; then I posed before my mirror in pure joy.

I was transfigured.

I know in my soul that form-fitting leotards are the fashion of my native planet: in the 'seventies, when spandex became popular and men and women sallied forth from health clubs in skin-tight attire, I felt less lonely on earth.

But Mom's design caused me problems in the crotch and on the buttocks. I felt (and I feel to this day), a reluctance to reveal either my genitals, healthy as they look, or the crevice defining my muscular glutes. I whispered to Dad.

"Mom, Clark loves his uniform but he's upset folks'll see his wiener and his hieney. —Can you fix it for him, Mom?"

No problem for my resourceful mother: she copied the cloth padding over the crotch-fronts of women's bathing suits to smooth my buttocks. In front she inserted a 1 x 3 x 7" strip of foam-rubber indented to match my genital profile. I felt she solved the problem behind; but I was too modest to display the healthy bulge out there in front. Mom stared at my body for a few minutes, and hit upon the red trunks that combine with the tactical pads to preserve my decency and minimize friction and wind resistance.

The next day she completed my cape; it felt a little showy and feminine to me, but Mom asked me to wear it for her and Dad, "You'll be *cold* up there in the sky, Clarkie."

I wear it with pride, feeling their loving arms as I don it.

Petroleum-based materials have enhanced the technology of sport and flight. My uniform has evolved within its basic image and structure, affording me the relief of wicking action when my exertions produce moisture. My frontal support is provided by a felt-upholstered styrofoam mold, reminding me of the polished, inlaid carrying-cases into which James Bond places the deadly tools of his trade. I allow myself these little private jokes about my colleagues.

Cherry Trinken heads up the PR department at WE: she's our highest-ranking female executive, and has Murd's ear on everything. PR is a solid profit-center: Cherry's art-franchises are a cash cow. Cherry carries the private numbers of the rich and famous in her sleek platinum palm pilot; she can get anyone anywhere anytime.

Her romances are legendary; WE achieved smashes with two authorized, two unauthorized, and three underground biographies, and produced a blockbuster movie that became a TV miniseries. She played herself in the film, wearing, when clad, her designer lines. The demand for more Cherry only grows.

Cherry Ltd.'s venture cap deal with WE is the stuff of speculation: punditry has it she outnegotiated Murd arranging financing and structuring ownership. "My equity position and risk exposure justify my faith in myself," she told *Barron's*. "I have superior financial taste to Martha Stewart's and Oprah's."

She made lewd advances at our first business meeting. As we gazed South towards the sun purple on the harbor from her corner office atop the WE (still known to some as the Empire State) building, I was saying, "You've had so many interesting relationships, Cherry. I cannot understand why you've not settled down to raise a family with one of your prominent escorts." My gaze was fixed on Lady Liberty as I spoke. A rhythmic pull on my cape interrupted, and Cherry, her little pink tongue licking her eponymous lips, whirled at me, wrapping her lucrative body tight inside the cape Mother made me.

"Ooooh, let's make babies of steel, Supe. Only you can be my man," she sighed in a voice all hot breath.

Thrusting her cantilevered left breast into my S symbol dead center, she gripped my hips in her left arm, tickling my pectorals and armpit with the perfect cerise nails of her jeweled right hand. She licked my ear and my neck—it tickled. Like a child with an aggressive babysitter, I felt helpless to contain waves of giggles as she sought my lips with hers and slid her shiny fingers with obvious intent across my trunks.

I executed a lightning head-fake to dodge the moist pink warmth. The sturdy materials of my cape trapped our combined body-heats. Her exploring hand found my crotch, but deterred by my molded plastic sheath, it darted about my pelvis like an evil lizard. My mature moral consciousness returned. My blood turned to molten lava burning from my agonized heart to my seething extremities. I wanted to kill Cherry; I longed to bellow out my hurt, to hurl her across the Metropolis and smash her against the broad brow of Lady Liberty. Her breathing was the roar of a bellows, an excruciating ringing echoed in my skull just as it echoed through my trauma with little Janey at Lazy Crick.

It was an effort as great as any I have exerted on earth to save Cherry from my rage. I strained and groaned. Mistaking my agony for arousal, she renewed her attack on my rear and my front simultaneously. I cursed her in my heart for desecrating Mom's work, but my mission would end in scandal if I killed her, no matter how malicious her assault upon my values and my person.

I took a deep cleansing breath.

"Cherry," I said, gently but firmly removing her hands from my thighs and detaching her breast from my sacred symbol, "I must not let personal feelings interfere with my mission. Your charms are most laudable; your breasts are magnificent, your face provocative, your hair-color beautiful, your jewelry dazzling, your makeup perfect, and your scanty business-suit alluring. But I curb my bodily functions with iron determination, and I must not distinguish male from female as I pursue my mission."

"Screw your mission," Cherry hissed, giving me the very look of dismissive disdain that hurt me so deeply throughout my formative years as an alien.

I took another cleansing breath, but still my rage seethed: the teak furnishings, the velour drapes, the priceless memorabilia were blended shades of red as if we were in a darkroom—Cherry the blood-red core. My x-ray vision supervened. Cherry was a skeleton, an armature of organs. I traced the ducts of her mammary glands as she eyed me shamelessly.

I strode to her terrace, the scene of so many famous power-gatherings, and flew away.

But I've got to hand it to Cherry: she summoned me back the next day through Murd's private line to my vibro-beeper. She was all business; we worked at the conference table by the lofty terrace as if nothing had happened in that very space. With the focused eagerness of the true entrepreneur, she outlined the PR campaign that has made us an item: we drop from the sky at big openings, the winds lifting her Cherrywear so that the cameras and the eyes of the surging crowds can shoot up her legs. She tells the media, "I just wish you could feel the power I feel," squeezing my bicep. I am happy to be needed to swell the WE bottom line.

Recently Cherry unveiled the proposal that generated this book, "Listen, Supe, I want you to start journaling. You owe your story to the world. It'll be a smash: *inside the man of steel!* Demographics great from top to bottom. Let's do it. I'll get you all the backup you need."

She has assigned a crack team of confessional ghosts, but I've asked her to hold them off until I am well into this new mission—for security reasons, I've said, but in fact I need to come to grips with talking about myself. I need to bone up on how to succeed at introspection.

Doing my research, I've asked Cherry how she conceived her blockbuster breakthrough business concept, MAMA, The Museums of Acceptable Modern Art, whose franchises have swept the nation's Fully Developed zones, taking the full 97% permissible market share of this high-end product.

"The Sixties, Supe. They taught me how to cash in. No Sixties, no MAMA."

Cherry attended Wellesley College with Hillary Clinton. "That was THE time of intellectual ferment and fulfillment, Supe, 'life, liberty, and the hot pursuit of happiness.' I wrote Hill's revolutionary graduation speech. I thought she'd delete 'passionate' and 'penetrating,' but no: she had the big-picture; she saw the connection between her personal needs and the country's future.

"God, it was great in college: a crucible of ideas and sensations, four years of cerebral orgasms. We knew early on that she'd do politics and I'd do media: the total power scene. We knew it was ours if we wanted it enough. That's what I tell the girls in business schools: just want it, girls. Dream it, want it, take aim, and go for it.

"The Sixties were *made* for Hillary and me—revolution after revolution—sex, drugs, race, clothes, poverty, Indians, image, women, posters, peace, rock, angels sweeping the campuses incubating tomorrow's—yes, today's!—leadership. Revolution is your inner GNP, Supe.

"The world needs to understand Cherry Trinken. I'm more than success and glamour; I'm a revolutionary.

"But early senior year, Supe, I had just simply the *worst* case of the existential fuck-its. Late Sunday morning I come back to Wellesley from one of those awful boozy parties with frat-boys at Williams in that icky building that looks like a hamburger, and I'm just a little sick of being Miss Most Pawed-Over. I've got all this work to do, this awful pile of books to turn into more fucking papers, and I just ask myself, *what is the meaning of all this meaning?*

"There I am, Sharon Trinkelstein of Queens, and the very first girl to go to Stevenhenge Academy off Park Avenue where they convert us into Episcopalians, and I've done the nose and I've worn the preppy wool skirts and learned good preppy manners and I've climbed the first summit of WASP power womanhood, I'm the big campus mover and shaker with Hill—but I'm running on empty, Supe, I mean I know it *all* but I don't *like* it anymore.

"See the stuff that makes them jump off the bridge at Cornell and hang themselves at Harvard, the pressure, the competition, the professors chuckling over your hick upbringing and your God while hiding books from each other in the library, profs on the make for corporate grants and not giving a shit about their students, promising me fellowships while staring up my skirt—hey, that's the game and I was born ready to play. No, it was deeper than that, Supe. It was that what the game was *about* that turned to ashes on me.

"I lost it Supe. Toking on Southern Comfort, angst up my wazoo, crying, laughing, yelling, 'Go deconstruct yourselves you assholes!' I took my new gut-strung Thunderclub from Head for Ladies and smashed the books all over the room. Helplessly mouthing, 'Oh, *crap* on you, Mr. Brown, I tore pages from *Life Against Death* and wiped my ass with them. My career, my life lay torn, shredded, a shitty heap on the floor, and all I had to show for all the pushing, pushing to get to this point was a perfect two-handed backhand to the spine of *Moby Dick*.

"But there was one book I had brought back from Paris that kept me ahead of everyone—*la Critique de la Critique de la*

Critique de la Critique. As I staggered and flailed through my despairing orgy of deconstruction, my favorite *mot* hit me like the voice of my future, *'The death of the author is the birth of the consumer.'*

"And, Supe, I just knew: at that moment when life was a crappy dumper full of beer cans, butts, sweat, bad breath and condoms, I knew my calling—turn art into money! I accepted the challenge: hey, the fine arts are the most boring thing around, *but already* museums were the highest society icon and painters considered great because they sold big! Nobody *liked* what they bought, any more than they liked opera. Like table manners, art and opera were middle-class self-torture, a weird offspring of Puritanism.

"What if I could give them something they'd like: they already felt they *should*—what if they *could*? They were rich; they deserved more than art was giving them. I vowed to give them the same happiness they got from power shopping.

"The rest is history, Supe: I climb the ladder, I become a trendsetter, I get capital, I launch MAMA #I with dear little Eddie Minksop on 57th Street in the atrium next to Nukee House, smack in the middle of New York culture—Warner World, Rock Center, the NBA Store, Von Umph Tower, Jeckyl and Hyde, Tiffany's. Then the bull market, MAMAs spreading like wildfire, WE buying in and the rest is history!

"So you see, Supe, feelings *matter*—Cherry without her Wellesley Crisis wouldn't be Cherry. That's the inner Cherry.—Have I helped you?"

Cherry was modest about her contribution to the art of management and marketing. The subject of countless B-school case studies, MAMA hit on a formula for delivering a product Fully-Developed consumers could count on: the reliable artist. MAMA artists are rigorously tested and quality-controlled. To qualify, they must Auto-Deconstruct. They submit the personal data that drives their creativity: DNA, sexual preference, religious affiliation, psychic profile, clothing-style, recovery history, significant relationships, political preference. These are run against the MAMA and WE databases for accuracy, and a general search of insurance and medical industry records initiated.

Should these check out, the artist submits a Style Preference Profile, detailing the subject-matter, degree of optimism, degree of differentiation from popular products, sexual appeal, level of iconoclasm, ease of installation (with consumer directions) as well as a one-paragraph authorized discussion and analysis-text, to assure consumers of the acceptability and importance of what they purchase. If this Profile tests well with income-qualified focus groups, the artist signs not only a Content Supplier Contract specifying the product specifications and the royalty percentages, but also a MAMA Non-Compete detailing the conditions, if any, under which he may produce original non-Profile material. Artists remain MAMA-authorized not only by upholding their agreements, but also by submitting quarterly financial data, medical data, relationship data, and blood samples.

A *Time* cover article, "Can this Woman 'Americanize' American Art?" heralded Cherry's crusade, and soon Madison Avenue, 57th Street, the Hamptoms, SoHo and TriBeca were experiencing astounding vacancy rates as the cream of the artistic world deserted their galleries to join her uptown and in suburbia. Suburban real estate agencies struggled when it became the rage for women bitten by the entrepreneurial bug to take advantage of liberal financing terms and break ground for Original MAMA franchise museums. Newspapers across the land created Art Sections featuring sales standings and exciting accounts of art-slams. Artists began to rival business heroes, athletes, and rock stars in the popular pantheon. Cherry was everywhere preaching the gospel of female empowerment through the arts.

"You see, Supe, the personal became a product in the 20th century, but until my breakthrough vision at Wellesley nobody knew how to make that product pay big time."

Cherry inspires me to believe I can make a contribution to the health of our society by writing about my Self. As I work, I am tortured by doubts—but Dr. Pill and Cherry teach me that light can rise from darkness.

2 LESSONS FROM MY YOUTH

I combat crime, and I always win. I've learned it's a mistake to fight sin; I fight crime, the crimes we Americans *know* are bad: I fight them, I beat them and I triumph over their perpetrators. You've all heard of me; I've done my level best to deserve the honors you've heaped on me. You've heard I might retire. It's true: I owe you my public a full explanation. I will explain my life, and hope you'll understand why I'm leaving. I am the man of steel, but I have feelings.

My father was proud of me. That means everything, making Dad and Mom happy. They had big, kind hearts—big as this land.

They didn't have it so easy with me. It's difficult for farmers to experience anything outside normal days and folks, much less adopt it and call it your own child, and by golly there I was dropped from another planet, and there they were with a child when everyone thought they were too old. They knew there'd be lots of talk. Their settled lives focused on crops, livestock, pets, and their fellow church-goers; they had accepted their shame, the Christian judgments on their childless hearth—suddenly a miracle dropped from the heavens. Me! They loved to tell me all the "funny stuff" they experienced with me: it comforts me to hear their dear departed voices from my audio workstation, to see their wholesome faces on my screen-saver. I crave their love, their approval, their guidance: the only audience I want anymore. I need their pure spirits here now in my time of trials—I must be strong and positive in their honor.

Mom and Dad always helped me when I failed to understand what was expected of me, especially at school. I do not permit my extra perceptions to trap me as they did when I was little and new on earth—at least not until recently. My parents couldn't know what I was feeling, they couldn't see what I was seeing, but they felt I was an upset and confused little guy, and they saved me and stuck up for me.

I outstripped other toddlers by miles. Space comprised the easiest three of my five dimensions; motion through it at any angle was a snap. I walked as soon as I wanted to, and my instinct drove me to reach my goals at once. Hills and stairs were fun. I laughed at my flabby chums begging their parents to carry them and steady them. My prowess angered my fellow-babies and nettled their parents, for whom walking was a competitive issue.

I was sensing intimations of my mission to this planet. When the babies' parents urged them, "Come on, it's easy. Stop that crying, you know you can do it!" —I stepped right in to show my chums their parents were right. I strode up the stairs and stood beside their parents with my big smile and my little arms open wide just like the grownups, but nobody appreciated my good example. My chums wept and screamed at me—that hurt; it hurt worse when their parents blamed *me* for their bratty nonsense and weakness. I was only there to help.

One hot sunny afternoon I strolled up the Lazy Crick rise with little Janey Velt. The Velts were our Quaker neighbors, Janey the youngest of seven. Lazy Crick ran down along their property into ours, and Dad and Daniel Velt dug irrigation trenches from it together until I got old enough to do it for them. Janey, her Mom and I were toddling up the hill through the alder grove marking the property line. Gusts up to 25 mph blew dust at us. Dappled cows ambled over to greet us. We emerged into the hot sun, and Janey stretched her little hands out to Mommie ahead, whimpering "Carryou Moomma, carryou!" I loved her cute little voice and her little curly bangs. I loved her even more than my faithful dog Ezra. I took her hand, swung it gaily, helping her right along with firm tugs. I was *there* for her; I felt so *good*, so thrilled to be such a good guy. Janey panted and sobbed, so I picked her up, cradling her across my chest, smiling into her face. She struggled, her little eyes wide over her chubby cheeks; she squealed louder and pee-peed and did something else in her diaper. Taking a firm grip on her biceps, I held her at arms' length. I must have squeezed her fat arms too hard: the next thing I knew her mother was holding little Janey and yelling down at me, her cries loud beyond any dimensions of sound I could endure, echoes rattling and banging in my small soft skull, and everything around resolved into hot red dots flying at me. I screamed back.

The ground shook, and the next thing I remember is Dad picking me up from the dust. My roars had driven away Janey's mother and all the Velt's cattle. Sobbing, Dad worked and worked to stop my bellowing, his chest heaving as he hugged and stroked me; he was more frightened than I was. Dust thrown up by the stampeding herd covered me, dirtying the cheery clothes Mom sewed for me. My eyes were scratchy with it. Dad shoved Ezra away from licking my face; the poor thing retreated whining with his black tail between his graying brown legs, causing me new spasms of fear and grief.

My native planet knows that sound is the fifth dimension. We were quiet and strong there, requiring no machines or technical devices to extend our physical and mental powers. We were strong listeners, in tune with each other, and with our planet. Puny and noisy, humans require loud appliances and weapons, which they call technology, to achieve what they call power.

As Clark I call the pain from earthly loudness a "migraine." In my real being I have learned to control the rage the noise-affliction unleashes in me, channeling the resultant excruciating restlessness into even greater exploits. You have heard that one particular element weakens me. Until today I have never revealed how earth's unconstrained, aggressive loudness pains me.

The first Quakers in our county, the Velts were isolated by their religion. Dan and Dad were close: they farmed as partners. Dan came by the house most nights. He rarely said a word. He never cut his black hair, or shaved his black beard. He liked to watch me play. Suddenly he'd laugh and slap his skinny knee when I did something unusual. His laugh would startle you: he'd be sitting there taciturn in his battered hat, carving some little toy for Janey or wolfing down a huge piece of pie, and suddenly he'd bark out through his bushy beard. Dad would say, "You OK, Daniel," and he'd say "Yep" and explode again. That night of my traumatic event with Janey he got down and played with me, barking again and again, letting me and Ezra pick the sawdust and crumbs from his beard until Mom stopped us. He'd stare and stare at me, but his gaze never embarrassed me like most grownup stares. He believed I was the coming of something, and told me he wanted to be there to see what would arrive. Perhaps Dan became close to me when, wandering about our fields with Ezra, I came upon him with his pants down, a knobby brown thing like a rope coming out of his pale behind, and I never told.

And so I entered school with unresolved formative relationships with my peers. School proved an agonizing trauma. The first-grade readers used a restricted vocabulary in odd combinations I never heard in daily life. Their copious illustrations were limited to a repetitious palette of pastel hues I never saw in real life. I couldn't decipher the pictures or construe the texts. I felt like an alien.

Following my perceptual heritage, I experienced the readers holistically, with deep looks, so that the words and images piled on top of themselves, causing humiliating episodes in class.

Mrs. Handy would write the words she thought difficult on the blackboard, and she'd demonstrate them with huge slow movements of her mouth. Then it was our turn, accompanied by her pointing to her tongue, teeth, palate and jaw to show us how to produce the sounds. I wanted to laugh at her funny working face, but all the other kids were imitating her so I tried to join in. My squelched laughter ruined my coordination, so I'd make foreign sounds and my classmates laughed at me. Then when we were reading out loud in turn, I'd be lost in my peculiar visual depths and say the words from pages ahead. Dick and Jane sounded crazy. The class squealed, giggled and pointed at me. The kind Mrs. Handy became just another grownup uncomfortable with me, straining to tolerate my disabilities. She discussed the merits of Special Ed with me and my folks.

A teaching assistant, Miss Batch, recorded a class; I read, "*Castor's glove oiled the well tumbled up the sunbeam the dog's spots star shower the hottest heat the dark bucket rolled Jill* (laughter)." Miss Batch, who reminds me of Lois, wondered if I was an authentic genius from the heartland, and I became her project. She told me I was "beautiful," that my words were poetry. She sent me to counselors with heavy rims on their glasses who used weird words on me and asked me dirty questions. They gave me tests with toys and puzzles and codes to crack, which confused me because I thought reading was my problem. I was so adept at the tests they thought I could be one of those idiot savants, but they had never heard of a mental *and* physical idiot like that.

Mrs. Handy loved her work; she was a progressive. She'd begin each school day by lining us up to kiss her on the cheek. She brought in her husband, a carpenter, to set up special projects for us. We spent happy weeks attaching walls of cardboard and rolled newspapers painted brown to a frame he built: we were doing a culture-unit on The Pioneers by creating a charming authentic log cabin replica. We brought in heirlooms from our attics to furnish it. We loved the taste of the white paste in the big glass jars, and we dumped gobs of it into each other's shirts. Mrs. Handy was tall: I was shocked to see her looming over Mom and Dad—to me the biggest people alive. She was pretty; she looked like a model from the Sears catalogue.

But after these creative units we returned to traditional learning, and to my troubles. To me the words on which we focused were empty: I did not yet think in words. My thoughts were images accompanied by a music I've not heard since, even on Broadway—images with trailing tails like comets; thinking was like being an orrery. My thoughts and my memories were tactile surround-sound screens showing teeming planets of meaning circling each other and themselves, and when I wanted to do an earthly verbal search in there, to do what Americans call thinking, I couldn't know how to limit my inner experience to something so pinched.

Miss Batch came out to the farm to understand my influences. Mom and Dad disappointed her: they lacked "authentic traditions;" our only book was The Bible, and we had no "folkloric" musical instruments like zithers or dulcimers or twanging saws. One day Miss Batch disappeared from school forever. I missed her; she was on my side like Mom. She wore long flowery dresses the way love-children did in the Sixties. Always clean of makeup, her face looked like a sugar-cookie.

Mom and Dad fretted over me until I achieved the strength and insight to give the school just exactly what it wanted. For during this momentous first grade I could *feel* myself growing both inside and out. I heard mothers and kids speak of "growing pains," heard parents embarrass kids exclaiming, "My how you've grown!" They made us ashamed, as if our whole bodies were public displays of something private. But I could feel myself growing not only physical strength but also *will power.*

Halfway through the first grade, after Sunday dinner during the Washington's Birthday break, I experienced the religious conversion that has sustained me throughout my mission: There was Dr. Norman Vincent Pill on the radio telling me I can win, I can do anything be anything own anything I want because I am a grain of mustard seed and I can plant myself and water myself from inside and I can grow to any height because my thoughts and feelings can switch from negative to positive. *And at that moment, hearing that show, they did!* A switch was turned, a button was pushed. The voice from the old wooden Philco was the authoritative narrator, the voice-over to the brand-spanking new newsreel of my life and spirit. A surging current of warmth flowed through my body and my brain. Negative complexes fell away like dead fingernails. Mom looked up from her needlework to say, "How that man does go on," and I knew then that she could never comprehend what I was experiencing—the decisive channeling of all my powers into will power, but I was nonetheless serene for I would make her proud. Daniel eyed me and nodded in silence. There is a deep religious current that pulses through These States, and at that moment in the first grade I plugged into it.

And so I knew now it was now only a matter of expecting the best of school, and my troubles would vanish, overcome by positive energy. And they did! Playing "Fish" with Mom, revelatory lightning struck: school wanted me to "go fish!" To do a search in my head, what teachers called learning, I need only flatten, shrink, and hush my orbiting mental images, reducing them to a silent simple picture like a fish-card, or even easier, like a spelling flash-card. The multiple dimensions of my spiritual heritage faded, fell away like scales. Learning became simple, easier than walking, the moment I gave up thinking. Dr. Pill energized my brain to play the game of school.

The number of useful, normal thoughts was small, their surfaces flat. Suddenly I could read one page at a time, focus on Dick and Jane in word and picture. From that Tuesday I was happy and made friends and got straight A's.

These were basic life-lessons one and two: reserve my super-powers and my vocation until earthly victims called for them; constrict my imagination to normalcy, so that I could function as an American. Number three was doing puberty and mastering my sex-lessons in the eighth grade.

I liked boys *and* girls, men *and* women. It was awkward for me to separate from the opposite sex and giggle about it like my buddies, but I worked at it. Some girls made me feel warm and happy, like small helpings of Mom. The boys I liked made me feel that I belonged, that I was normal, like Dad. When I didn't like a girl or a woman I felt nauseous. When I didn't like a man I felt a prickly heat, a restlessness. I experienced no attraction to doing to girls all those disgusting things the boys told me about, nor did I want to mature and sire little ones the way Dad explained it and demonstrated Barney the bull doing it to me in the paddock—especially since Dad had not sired me.

I struggled to find the positive in the pubic rituals my classmates observed. It was awkward work for me to crack dirty jokes about the girls and to tell loud lies about sex-things I'd done to them—I couldn't work myself up, not matter how hard I tried, to share that obsession with my friends. I wrote a letter to Dr. Pill asking for guidance through these sensitive issues, and received a kind, beautifully-printed reply about the sanctity of the body.

The next day I mounted the school steps in phalanx with my buddies, systematically imitating their swagger, pitching in to shout dirty words, cackling grunting and roaring towards the girls gathered at the top of the steps *shit look at that Janey Velt bitch huh, man those bumpers, I'll bet you've been over in* her *barn eh huh Clark huh? fuck yes shes got a very well-developing pair of mam erbitchin knockers we go way back huh huh aah haa haa har mmhMMMuhcool ohfuckin yeahman*. From giggly huddles beneath the American flag snapping in the breeze by the concrete portals, girls stole glances at us, nudging and whispering, scornfully chewing and popping Juicy Fruit at us *squish squish pop pop pop*. —And then and there on a crisp autumn morning before the doors of Rural HS 23, I was granted my sexual revelation: Our stances—our aggression and braggadocio, the girls' simpering and scorn—freeze-framed and morphed in my mind. The girls' breasts and hips grew, and they became actresses in soap operas and guests revealing themselves on a talk show; the boys' hair grew wilder or their skulls were shaven; their muscles and bellies filled in, and they too looked like soap actors and daytime panelists—a few like wildly-degenerate rock idols.

And I realized the secret of American sex: puberty sanctifies and focuses the human need to show off. Like school, sex is a simple game with a few repetitive moves. Already in middle school I was the fastest and most powerful man ever known on the planet; it was cinchy for me to perform feats beyond any boy's wildest show-off dreams. So my only problem would be holding back girls attracted by my prowess, but that would be *so* much more pleasant than ostracism and frustration.

I take a private, quiet satisfaction in myself and my feats that is far more potent than the pleasures humans get from their sex-acts. I'm certain of this, for often my work entails surveiling them doing sex. I am proud to say that I have never had an erection.

The warmth I feel for women, especially Lois, impels me to even greater exploits. Likewaise, my brotherhood with men, and its opposite, my kinetic anger, spur me on. My other me, Clark Uberman Kent, is the confused, sensitive. awkward semi-alien appearing to be a normal productive American. His identity traces back to the traumas of these life-lessons. On the front steps of Rural HS 23, invisibly to my preoccupied classmates, I completed my transition into maturity, transfigured again and ready to accept my mission. My identity was formed, my powers in place. I would thenceforth grow serenely, amassing and processing the information I need to fulfill my mission. You know the exploits resulting from this process. My publicity has focused on my physical exploits; few realize the extent to which I embody this millennial information age. This book will demonstrate the broad range of my lesser-known talents. But please do not think I am over-proud: the information revolution is, like laying railroad tracks, a trivial game compared with the insight and imagination I forswore in Mrs. Handy's class. Cyberspace is trash compared to the wonders of our universe.

I am aware of only One in human history greater than I, and like my parents and Dan Velt, I worship His mighty example, and His insights into life's issues.

I chuckle at the paltry accomplishments of the sports heroes Americans worship—but the Scriptures chasten me:

star athletes are my little brothers, and I nod my approval. Michael Jordan died recently in Las Vegas, sadly neglected after serving out his declining years as an itinerant crowd-greeter at the worldwide Von Umph casino empire. I joined his modest cortege, stars of lesser magnitude, escorting his coffin through Forest Lawn. We threw a pile of authentic nets from each of the 200 hoops of the World NBA onto his final resting-spot, and I burned the Nukee swoosh into his sculptured headpiece—Michael eternally getting air—with the heat of my eyes.

3 A BLOW

"Clark, how do you feel about oral sex?" Lois asks me at lunch today.

I know why she's asking. Long salamis and globular cheeses dangle down to our heads. We're eating at a deli whose sanitary practices I can accept. As Lois chatters, I analyze the salamis and their provenance: pigs from the vast North Carolina factory ruining the regional aquifer, grain filler from a huge rat-filled load Cargoil sold Particular (formerly General) Foods as hi-grade wheat 2 years ago in a hedged transaction that made both sides feel they scored big. Cargoil Sales dumped the bad grain it got past the barge inspectors; the trader at Particular Foods discounted his insider knowledge PF planned huge buys for a new health-pizza product, driving up the premiums on all grain derivatives. The commodities merchant at Salomonic, lightening with this trade the unauthorized long position he took buzzed on cocaine, messengered both sides two boxes of ersatz Cohabitiba Cuban cigars from a load of ordinary smokes hijacked in North Carolina by the Mafia group helping the CigarEsq cigar-bar chain avoid duties on the identical materials it sells cigar aficionados at graduated prices repackaged under the prestige labels Orale I-IV.

The deal ticketed, the traders lighted up in synch on a video conference, saying, "It doesn't get any better than this... Yeah, it doesn't get any better than *this!*...Oh man you're right, it just *doesn't* get any better than this."

The strings tying these hung meats were hijacked for the salami-maker in Long Island City by the same gang, easy pickings from a stranded rickety truck that contained a year's worth of natural fibers shipped from a WE Foundation African-American enterprise in South Carolina to which the government proudly lent and which tourists solemnly visited to see what the pr called "folk capitalism." The strings' final destination was the one remaining wooden dock on Long Island where the three remaining Long Island fishermen patched their nets, another part of the WF Authentic America Enterprise network of tourist attractions. I love the brochure for this Montauk attraction, "Hard-bitten Yankee Salts." The fishermen are forbidden to use sunscreen, so that their faces look etched by the elements.

These are the extra-Manhattan or Manhattan-benefiting trickle-up crimes with which I have compacted with overt and covert municipal, federal, and global police authorities and client governments to co-exist, but it is my standard operating procedure to stay abreast of mob practice.

"Clark, *answer me*, you're daydreaming again. Don't avoid the question. Tell me your opinion on oral sex."

Normal days, I go to the office. I take the slow way: I drive. For me an auto is child's-play; maybe this is why humans stick to their internal combustion through the gray air, the frustration and death: they are acting out infantile fantasies of control, mastery and independence. I look ahead through the traffic-pattern; I calculate my arrival-time time at the *Daily World's* parking lot down to the second. The traffic spotters on World All-News are behind by 43 minutes. It amuses me to see my fellow-commuters fly into rages over this simple problem in classical physics they refuse to solve by putting more body-volume into large-volume vehicles running on lower-friction tracks. But I understand efficient public transit could be a crack or weak spot into which Big Government could force its insidious wedge.

Today I park at 8:56:07, did the 11 miles in 1:47:49, 23 seconds faster than my mean. The crowd's body- pressure on me in the WE lobby—an imprecise gauge—tells me I'll be at work in the City Room at 9:04.

9:05 I sense an extreme and distended facial movement at the far end of the vast humming room. I lock onto Brian O'Brien, the City Editor. Normally growling gruff directives by now, he's wearing a silly grin behind his huge, paper-strewn desk, his office door-uncharacteristically closed. His trademark half-cigar (a smelly American product) is wagging like a dog's clipped tail. I am appalled to see Sally Sling (born Sarah Slepinsky), who openly flaunts her illicit relationship with Sal Mafficante, number one crime boss, unzipping his fly. She has him backed up against his pride and joy, the *World* Wall of Fame, where trophies and plaques for reporting excellence and civic contributions punctuate framed photos of everyone who has contributed to the building of our Metropolis. I am in many of the photos. Civic tours of the building take Brian from his hectic schedule to expound the glories and trophies. But now the famous shot of me, Brian and Mayor Hussell re-opening the Brooklyn Bridge is aslant next to Brian's deep-red head: blood has rushed to suffuse every inch of him above his open collar, from his jiggling dewlaps to his mottled pate. Sally's left hand cups his right buttock, her index finger pointing into his anus; she's darting her tongue into his ear like an evil snake as her right hand, flashing with rock-size diamonds and rubies, plunges into his pants.

Her trademark bared-fang silver fox furs, lying at their feet, seem to snarl at the shocking sight. She calls Brian her lox, her cheese, her bagel. She pulls out his pink-purple male member, which impresses me with its size, color and curvature, and she kisses and licks it. I'm calculating the best thing for me to do when I see Lois walking straight down the central aisle with her glasses on and a huge dossier hooked under her right arm like a football, and I know she's onto something big she's got to let the Chief know. She throws open the wide doors that allow Brian to stare down the City Room at all of us and yell at whomever he needs.

Lois cries out, "Holy shit! What are you *doing*, Brian?" She drops her dossiers with a thump.

Brian groans. His penis is pointing at Lois, at all of us down the gigantic room. Throbbing activity halts; we're still as a morgue. Sally rises from her knees slowly, pulls up her shoulder straps, and shakes her bosoms at Lois. I can see the conical bags of silicone in those breasts, the little clamps on her ovaries. I can see the lines where cartilage and bone have been cut from her nose and cheeks, fat sucked from her chin. The media call her the Foxy Femme Fatale.

"You're gonna regret this, Lane." Sally stalks by Lois in her stiletto heels. Her short skirt clings to her strong buttocks, showing her muscular legs. "I told Brian about you. Word is out, weirdo. Watch your back, bitch!"

Sally yanks a big goon I've ignored from behind his *WE Daily OnLine Gaming Form* in the front lobby, and drags him into the elevator, her fox fur glaring at us from her bare shoulders. The receptionist stays busy as ever taking the calls we always get from everywhere in the Metropolis. She is trained to notice nothing, her polite voice continues its singsong...

"Dammit, Clark, it can't take you all day to decide to order your turkey with lettuce on white bread. Answer me."

"I'm not well-informed about it, Lois."

"Yeah, yeah, I know you: you're wondering if it's a bad thing; if it's less of a health hazard than genital intercourse; if a married man like Brian gets it, is he committing adultery. And of course you'll never bother to think about how a woman like Sally came to be what she is, you'll just see her as an evil seductress. —Well? Anything to offer?"

"I told you, Lois, I'm not an expert on sexual subjects. That's not my beat. Would you like me to put someone onto a project? Do we have a story?"

"Do we have a *story*? Clark, are you the only one in the building who doesn't understand what happened in Brian's office today? Why do you think Sally Sling did it, Clark?"

"Just what did Sally Sling do, Lois?"

"Shit Clark, you're hopeless. Eat your fucking turkey."

But now I'm wondering about my email: I am getting obscene threats addressed to me as "Clark Cunt" from a classroom site in Forest Hills. I've meant to let the guidance department out there know. And I'm a little depressed by my command appearance before Rick Hussell and the CSC.

"Lois, let's see a show tonight! A musical will cleanse your mind of this sick stuff. This season Broadway is just pure positive uplift. Which one suits your fancy?"

"Oh, Clark, I don't know why I waste my time with you, except you're so sweet. Someday I'll find myself a normal man I can trust. You'll have to do for now.

"But I wonder why Sally's so angry with me..."

Lois and I see the new hit *Starved into Happiness*, affectionately known as "Los Mis" and "Mis 2," about a tribe in South America burned out of its rainforest by an American crew building a superhighway from a megastripmine. The terror of the first act is dazzling: smoke envelops the audience, and the savages run yelling and singing up and down the aisles among us, regroup in a chorus downstage, and move us to tears with the hit "Carry On" as the smoke lifts to reveal them in their ragged but colorful native garb:

We can't see our future
Our lives are gone
But we'll just carry on.

Lois and I hold hands, happily letting the stoic wisdom of the native Americans sink in.

The Chief meets by a tractor with the Foreman of the muscular American work-crew that has thrilled the ladies with so many hits on MTV Upscale. He's never seen a white man, and he feels the Foreman's muscles repeatedly, and the Foreman appreciates the chief's hunting-gear, particularly a long spear that the Foreman holds awkwardly but the Chief wields with ease. The muscles and the spear kindle mutual masculine respect where before there had been only bitterness and suspicion. These two real men can show initiative, and they have beautiful tenor voices for their duets about the future. The media call them the "Two Tenor Hunks." Their voices climb the register as they vision their way towards hope.

Then the Chief explains it all to the tribe, which is camped out by a dirty river that has infected them and is causing a couple of older squaws to die. Suddenly he is challenged by the malignant and ugly Bad-Eye, who wants to kill the pale gringos with venomous arrows, but he defeats him in a fair fight so intense it carries into the audience like Wrestlemania. Relieved, the sick old squaws resume their swan-songs, in which they prophesy a future filled with visitors made possible by the noise-monsters, as they poetically call the giant tractors that bulldoze in loud grandeur onstage courtesy of Caterpillage, again bringing tears to Lois' and my eyes, tears of sadness and pride.

A ragged band of protesters mars the sidewalk amenities of each show, offended by the term "squaw," but WE Broadway's Columbia University ethnographer has ruled in favor of accurate language.

In the last act the muscular Foreman, clad in a white medical robe cut off at the shoulders, brings medicines, water purifiers, and staggering armfuls of powdered food in time to save two sick starving babies whose adorable mothers sing wonderful duets carrying them about the stage in their bright papooses—for me the climax of the whole play is when Little

Brown-Eyes, played by Mary Mermaid, catches the papoose of her friend, Little Kind-Heart, who swoons from emotion and hunger at the end of their duet, saving the baby from landing on its cute little black-haired head. I am so entranced by the play I almost rescue the baby myself. I love the Great White Way.

The final chorus: a pioneer tourist's Sports Utility Vehicle is upstage center, and the tourist-family before it in safari outfits, their stage-business to cherish their historic purchases from the now fully-dressed tribe. The happy natives are arranged to frame the pilgrims in a receding V. The Chief, who brandishes the new Orale V cigar premiered on this stage, along with his trusty spear, bounds to downstage center at the V's symbolic jointure. He salutes a clean, successful future, and before the curtain rings down, when you can scarcely believe how wonderfully everything has turned out, the huge silhouette of the muscular Foreman vaults to the hood of the Sports Utility Vehicle with his chainsaw, the audience irresistibly drawn to passionate applause and assent as he joins the final bars of the climactic swelling of this harmonic vision of New Age ethnic and ecological harmony, and a screen appears upstage revealing the newsreel of the future they sing, the prophetic squaws reviving magically to bless in ecstasy generations of cute tribal children going dutifully to clean prefab schools tended by saintly-looking nuns who bend over these precious ignorant souls in utter kindness.

Lois is much calmer when I take her home.

But I have a painful nightmare: I am flying across Queens, the vector I normally take on my way home, and I am happily admiring the houses of Forest Hills. My face is a happy relaxed smile; the air in my face is cool. I allow myself to soar with the air-currents. But the air heats, and I cannot maintain my altitude. I am trapped in a hot downdraft that becomes a six-lane highway of air with a familiar stench I can't identify, a down-curved plane leading directly to the screen of a computer in front of which a freckled boy with large black-rimmed glasses smiles menacingly. He wears a ratty check sweater. He uses a toy in my shape as his mouse, with which he clicks an icon of me. I disappear into the screen, into red dots that sear my skin, and I shatter into glass fragments scraping themselves.

I awake at 3:07 AM, my head exploding.

4 WORLD HISTORY

I report metropolitan politics for the *Daily World*, one of the prestige properties of Rupert Murd's World Enterprises Plc, known everywhere as WE. Many distinguished newspapers and journalists contributed to New York City's history, and it was a climax of this illustrious tradition when Mr. Murd purchased the *New York Times* and its affiliated enterprises in 2001, completing his consolidation of New York journalism under *The World*. At the ceremony with young Sulzburger he proclaimed, "This is *the* crown jewel in my Global Info empire. I am humble but yet proud to have purchased this piece of history. I will treat it with the respect it deserves."

Since that deal, New York City's print journalism has spoken with one authoritative voice; the citizens of the Metropolis know what they need to. *The Daily World* has incorporated the hallowed motto, "All the news that's fit to print," and made it reality, thanks to Murd.

WE's empire, earth's largest in market capitalization, is divided into three global business lines: Information, Entertainment, and Technology. Global World Information encompasses book, newspaper and magazine publishing, both physical and online. It manages chains of private and semi-private schools, and all materials related to scholastic enterprises. We are grateful to our trusted consultant Michael Milkem, who guides and inspires us to wring profits from education. Our Milkem Colleges of Free Enterprise are crucial to building the business and political leadership of the future. These collegiate cash cows, campuses thriving in every Fully-Developed U.S. economic zone, invest primarily in and focus their management talent on their sports programs and complexes—creating motivated, competitive cadres of alumni donors and assuring a stream of profits through synergies with Global Entertainment we capitalize into ever-more aggressive plant-and-capacity-expansion programs. Many an MCFE dissertation or faculty research project germinates a successful product or department at Global Info or WE GTech.

It was my privilege to fly the gilded *M* to the crown of the arch atop the Cathedral Parkway entrance to the state-of-the-art Milkem Wing of the Columbia School of Anatomical Cosmetology that replaced Morningside Park in 2003. Within months of its heralded opening the treasured entrepreneur underwent the premier Total Pelvic Replacement, a procedure now so widely-accepted and profitable that persons of means eagerly sign onto our three-year waiting list, paying a six-figure retainer for the privilege. Cameras in the OR captured the premier for a breathless world, filling us in on the illustrious deeds of Mr. Milkem, and revealing the identity of the anonymous donor, a male dancer at Chippendales who, after his conversion to The Assembly of God, decided to eliminate temptation by downscaling his charms. It was a miracle of personal and financial serendipity that Mr. Milkem's cranial hair re-appeared during his recovery.

Our educational plants enjoy tax-favored status, thanks to the landmark opinion legal scholars agree is the crowning achievement of the Reintwist Supreme Court, in Palo Alto Public Schools vs. Milkem & Milkem, a decision smashing all artificial barriers between public and private enterprise, a decision with economic implications scarcely limited to education. Hedge funds holding long positions in WE futures cashed in as the momentous decision was being read.

Global Entertainment includes all consumer media—museums, theme parks, newscasts, historic sites, national parks, movies, nature preserves, television, plays, financial bulletins, rock concerts, and music—plus online and virtually-real versions of each. Disney Enterprises, acquired in 2001, accounts for 73% of the ebitda of this Division, and attaching the Disney name to a laggard national park or a risky play assures its success. Consumers, especially those in Fully-Developed or Pre-Conditional economic zones, know they can trust products backed by an authentic blue WE Disney label to provide wholesome, satisfying stimulation.

Global Entertainment managed our book-publishing portfolio until the education-business in Global Info took off following what Lois calls the Supreme Decision. Murd and Milkem grabbed immediately for the potent synergies inherent in schoolroom texts and materials as brand-loyalty builders, deploying content management and advertising to instill irreversable positive responses to WE in young minds.

WE GTech is led by the dynamic Rick Hussell, scion of New York's dominant political dynasty. The financial media predict Rick and Cherry will duke it out to succeed Murd. Rick's major impact on WE has been through the CSC, the Content Synchronization Committee, a state-of-the art digital war-room that monitors each byte of WE content to assure its consistency with our sponsors' advertising messages.

WE GTech is a profit center, franchising its knowledge, applications, codes, and equipment to governments and businesses whose prosperity it is our mission to assure. GTech's motto captures our tight alignment with our clients: *Make your problems ours*. GTech combines consulting with hardware and software, Murd having bought the Anderson and McKinsey consulting empires for use as facilitators when he acquired IBM, Apple, Compaq and the remnants of the Baby Bells in 2002. GTech consults with Macrosoft, but Bill Grates and Rupert Murd, during their historic televised bargaining session assembled in 2003 at Camp David by President Borebush, facilitated by Henry Kissinger and 11 Nobel Laureates in Economics, known popularly as the "Big 12" and called by *The Daily World*, "conceivably the most distinguished deliberative body assembled in recorded history," hammered out a Chinese Wall assuring they will remain relentless but respectful competitors. They pledged to observe the spirit and the letter of the Pro-Trust Laws of 2001 crafted by the President to assure global the triumph of free enterprise despite the perils of foreign competition.

Murd and Grates waged thrilling bidding-wars for the Louvre, the Forbidden City, and many other historic properties, illustrating the President's wisdom, and riveting the consumer public's attention. I was downcast when Grates won the Louvre by promising Paris and the Sorbonne exclusive rights to all improvements, upgrades, and trans-media reproductions of its contents, as well as insider access to the Bettman archive and monumental donations to their endowments; but when I flew Lois on an island-hopping jaunt across the Pacific to cover and celebrate Murd's victorious re-opening of the Forbidden City as a Disney Historic Theme Park, complete with the friendly Oriental dragon-characters Chow Mick and Chow Min, I was once again amazed and inspired by our leader's vision.

To Rupert Murd it is no surprise that the largest enterprise on the planet is ruled by an Australian whose fortune became a potent capitalist force in Great Britain: "Capitalism is transnational. I call it 'enterprise unbound,'" he likes to say. And he'll add with that famous glint in his hawk eyes, "Adam Smith, Malthus, and Darwin were Brits. The sun never set on our empire and never will."

World Enterprises cooperates with government at all levels. Suffering entrepreneurs no longer feel shackled, abused and depleted by insensitive bureaucrats and by paper. The climactic conclusion to the tension between business and government was heralded by President Borebush, as he pledged during his historic acceptance speech at the Millennial Democratic convention: "My work over the last 8 years to streamline and downsize government may have gone unnoticed. Many in fact have called it boring. But let me tell you my friends, it has paved the high road to an action that I will initialize within an hour of waking up after my Inaugural Ball, should I be so blessed by you our wonderful people, and I just feel I will with your help and God's and Tupper-Ann's—I will labor unrelentingly and unremittingly with both Houses of Congress to abolish the Internal Revenue Service, replacing it with a simple collection service through your local bank of choice, and I will enact one simple flat tax for all enterprises and individuals, reserving the complexities of credits and deductions for corporate legal departments where they belong, not on the shoulders of the striving middle classes that make this nation strong and vibrant.

"No more will a federal Big Brother come between Americans and their precious dollars. I have cut that federal Big Brother Bully down to size, with my quiet, thankless, unappreciated but relentless Streamlining Initiative. I know all that Big Bully's Tricks! He can't escape George Borebush, folks, oh no no he can't!

"Our engines of wealth drive us down the information superhighway at mach speed and warp torque to be the great people and nation we can be in the new millennium. Let us go forth around the globe now and forever, let us all be all we can be!"

That statesmanlike masterstroke of compromise with the deep principles of the Republican opposition assured the President's overwhelming victory. Our hearts and minds were captured by a politician who could stand tall and block politics from clogging the engines of free enterprise. His surprise opponent, Strom DeLye—the only Republican running in the primaries with legal aliens as nannies, a spotless sexual and substance history, a mammoth PAC, a sincere enthusiasm for gun-owners, and strong evangelical Christian credentials for office—made eloquent denunciations of the many left-wing homosexuals who advised Mr. Borebush. But all pundits and the polls and at times even DeLye himself acknowledged that Borebush and his handlers and pollsters had executed a smashing coup assuring the overwhelming stream of contributions leading to his election and re-election.

Mr. DeLye sits on the Board of Directors of WE, an historic first by a former Speaker of the House, wrought by the Pro-Trust and the Tax Reform Acts of 2001, which he and the President crafted and enacted with only one dissenting vote in both houses—a gay labor sympathizer sent to richly-deserved retirement in the 2002 primaries. DeLye was there when the President signed the Acts with 30 pens, symbolizing his prediction that the Dow Jones Average would never again drop. During the ceremony Borebush amazed the press with his fluent grasp of economics and finance, asking a triumphant Milton Friedman whether the current equity markets demonstrated a classic head-and-shoulders chart pattern, and nodding with informed concern when Friedman assured him that the only danger to our prosperity is rising wages and goaded the Fed to be vigilant lest labor advances destroy our hard-won prosperity. The President's invitation to Friedman was a sign of his magnanimity: his aides had lobbied to make Borebush *Time's* Man of the Year, but the designation went to the economist who has captured best the spirit of our free-market age—a spirit synthesized and powerfully distilled in the global broadcast of his epochal Gifford/Pinochet Lecture series at Harvard University on all public and educational channels.

Truly the Supreme Decision and the Acts are the second American Revolution.

Murd assures the harmonious global cooperation of his enterprises with national, state and local governments by hiring qualified former politicians, civil servants, diplomats, generals, and colonels into WE Corporate Public Relations, run within Global Info as a profit center by Cherry. These dignitaries assist our aggressive public-sector acquisition program, as Murd pounces on government entities unable to cope with the streamlining dictated by the revenue shrinkage the President unleashed. When waves of urban and rural public schools closed, he stepped in selectively to acquire their plants, equipment and labor for Milkem's ed start-ups. When public parks deteriorated, he snapped them up as building-sites for GTech, or invested his private wealth developing them with Donald Von Umph.

Global Entertainment profited too: Murd's first coup was his purchase in 2002 of two miles of the Passaic River, the Falls, and the moldering remnants of Alexander Hamilton's enterprises from the bankruptcy trustees of the City of Paterson, New Jersey. Market analysts were slow to grasp how a neglected inner-city landscape could turn a juicy profit as the Premier Urban Theme Park, for they underestimated the nostalgia in Suburbia for our cities, a nostalgia as lucrative for WE as our devotion to the Wild West.

The main attraction is a three-dimensional urban gang violence and school terrorism ride, presented in a tasteful environment demonstrating moral lessons to children and adolescents. The Hamilton-Burr duel ride, featuring virtual renditions of Burr's many glamorous conquests, is number two. The Paterson Falls, colorized day and night by lasers and Jersey-made dyes, an easy drive from all eastern demographic concentrations, has all but eclipsed rival Niagara Falls (owned by a downsized but still-feisty Sony) as an attraction for lovers.

Murd's choice of New Jersey for investment was serendipitous: a bipartisan flood of that state's politicians proposed a creative medley of money-making schemes to WE PR. Soon public figures from across the country and around the globe joined these New Jersey pioneers in presenting projects and resumes. WE PR has been the subject of many business-school case studies. Like our academic departments, it serves as a cutting-edge research function, bubbling up a constant stream of entrepreneurial creativity.

For in the new paradigm of the Information Millennium, the focus of modern enterprise cannot be solely or even primarily to develop new markets, it must refresh the appetites of consumers in existing markets. Murd's harnessing PR as his engine of growth is his deepest insight into how to make vast corporate empires ever- vaster. Here's how it works:

The WE braintrust recognizes three global stages of consumer development, *Emerging Markets* (like East Timor or the South Bronx, which we leave to small local businesses we monitor as takeover opportunities), *Pre-Conditional* (like Akron or urban Mexico, into which we place our basic product-set), and *Fully-Developed* (like Manhattan, Shaker Heights or Hong Kong, towards which we direct the full force of our communications resources, and to which we sell our upscale product-sets).

The Fully-Developed consumer's appetite for products is infinite. Marketing theorists who postulate "saturated" or "mature" markets are ignorant of human psychology in the English-speaking world.

WE's final epochal marketing coups were creatures of crisis. One Friday at the height of the electoral season of 2000, Murd was subjected to a series of grueling hearings by reformers of the left and right: Republicans suspicious of foreigners, Democrats suspicious of global employers targeted this Australian magnate living on a Hollywood hill with his young Asian consort—timing their hot verbal probes for maximum exposure on the weekend news packages. That evening in his suite at the Capital's Haye-Watney, grasping a cut-glass tumbler of his private-reserve aged and bonded single-malt Glumliver, Rupert Murd exploded at his quaking braintrust, "Blast this bloody nonsense! I own these bitches and bastards. Every one of those pigs swills from my PAC. I don't take this crap from my staff; why should these candy-asses be any different? I'll show these flatulent hogs who's boss."

And so he bought the ten largest lobbying law firms on K Street. The American Bar Association's rigorous code of ethics limited his position in each firm to 41%, and the Association required that Murd decree an insurmountable Chinese Wall between WE Legal and the tripartite WE Corporate—a decree with which Murd was eager to cooperate, for it assured that WE Corporate's deliberations could remain privileged from WE Legal.

After this stunning coup, Rupert Murd owned a controlling interest in the retired lawmakers, regulators and military heroes of Washington, and a controlling influence on the active dignitaries.

Finally, he bought Ovid and Gaffem Ltd., the prestigious agency contracting for the speaking-tours, autobiographies, movies and media bookings of public figures. Privately, Murd indulges in Down-Under humor, referring to his dealings with the political world as "getting into my pimp-mobile." He enjoys negotiating contracts with statesmen personally. During his first session with George H. W. Bush, who was eager to upgrade his fees for speaking in Asia on behalf of the Reverend Moon from six to seven figures like Ronald Reagan's, he puzzled the Yale-educated Texan by calling him "Shagpoke." Leaks of the session caused consternation in Bush's former home, the CIA, which frantically searched its records lest Murd was exposing the code name for ethnic cleansing operations in El Salvador, Guatemala and Panama.

WE's dynamism has caused social as well as business and political revolutions. The traditional cream of the social crop hesitated to embrace MAMA, Cherry's revolutionary contribution to the fine arts sector. *Town and Country* devoted and entire issue to the questions of status it raises, and to the agonizing reappraisals of traditional artwork portfolios it wrought. Some of the nation's toniest families were obliged by their traditions and values to join, with a sad scent reminiscent of another *fin-de-siecle*, the well-chronicled "Flight to Opera." Rococo, the sensitive scion of the oil-refinery Blotter dynasty of Manhattan and Texas, penned in response a phillipic to the *T&C* editor, quoted repeatedly in the upscale media and in *God's Club*, essays on golf and life by John Upright:

What has this world come to when a Monet is no longer a Monet, a man a man, and a woman a woman? We Blotters uphold known and accepted standards in clubs, schools, viewpoints, neighborhoods, foreign countries, people, islands, habits. We've taken on the burden, worthily we trust, to uphold these standards. If what we've valued is broadcast, nay, noised abroad willy-nilly, we must abdicate—and we cannot answer for the consequences to society.

Master marketer that she is, Cherry welcomed the brouhaha, pointing out that the traditional American aristocracy became useless when the Cold War ended: "A society no longer under attack needs no white knights from Yale and the CIA to go on crusades."

Murd, whose tastes run to sentimental Irish ballads and Cole Porter, finds the Fight to Opera piquant. Applicants for coveted diplomatic postings are now forced to prove their mettle by enduring the *Ring Cycle* and writing detailed memos on its performance.

He is confident and serene in the face of the righteous liberals who lament his merger of government, the special interests, and the Third Estate. During his famous "Sixty Minutes" profile, he told an indignant but charmed Leslie Stale,

"Now Leslie, take a look at the facts. The dollar-vote ratio is way north of a thousand-to-one, way north. The marginal votes we're after, the winning votes, cost at least that. Add up the expenses: politicians' salaries while they run (and that's what they do, Leslie, they run), media consultants' fees (way up there, I know, heh-heh), early and mid-campaign media buys, polling and focus-group operations and staffing, traditional campaign staffing and materials, T&E at a dignified level, cash for miscellaneous persuasive payments (you like the way I put that, Leslie, you see I'm not such a foreign barbarian), and, most important of all, tactical over-budget media attacks and counter-attacks on the eve of the vote leading to campaign deficits that cause the winners to go back to the trough as soon as they're elected, or become lobbyists if they lose.

"Joe Voter hasn't got the economic horsepower to buy those marginal votes—I do.

"I have an enterprise to protect; thousands, hundreds of thousands of people around the globe depend on WE. I provide and protect their livelihoods. Why should I let the future of WE be blown around by political winds—please note, Leslie, I did not say windbags. (*Camera zooming in on his famous poker-faced twinkle.*)

"What I do is more important than what any politician does. Business leaders are global; politicians are national, parochial. Why shouldn't I have a say while they're in office, and why shouldn't I reward them when their race is run and they've hung it up from fighting the good fight?"

5 THE PLOT

It will put her in hot water with Brian and the CSC, but Lois will pursue the Sling matter. She'll let it cool a bit first.

"That woman is venomous, Clark. She scares me. I don't want Sal and his crew after me. I'll cool it a week or two. I'll do a quick New Age-er. I'll heal some."

Lois is famous. In our information era, the authoritative and piquant personalities delivering the news achieve higher ratings than the figures making it. Lois is the lone print reporter adorning this pantheon of news-managing newspeople. I give her exclusives on my missions to help keep her up there.

She has big brown eyes that grow wider and little dimples that pucker and grow pink as she pursues her investigations. I love Lois; she's the sister I never had. She reminds readers of the old days of crusading, influential journalism. With a profitable gesture to nostalgia, WE PR projects her "muckraker" image. I know I'm in the presence of greatness as I join Lois in the fight for truth and justice, but whenever I compliment her, she teases me, "Hey, I'm the WE pet liberal: liberals are harmless; we perform noble gestures to make you feel good. Shit, it's a job."

I love her enthusiasm. She performs yogic stretches and deep breathing maneuvers at her workstation. She cries over injustice, and defies wrongdoers. Her figure is fully feminine, but willowy and supple. She dresses in excellent taste, eschewing the trendy. The men she dates never meet her standards, and she takes her breakups hard. She weeps and rails, "Yeah, yeah, I *know* I've got to go through this fucking process of mourning over the dickhead; yeah, yeah, I've got to go *through* the process, not around it—how about a little casual sex to help me out, Clark?" Suddenly she'll emerge from her funk with a shout to the City Room: *"Watch out guys, I'm going for your balls!"*

This spring, after dumping a "dreamboat," she organized the "Big Swinging Uterus Squad." Lois and her sisters grabbed their crotches dramatically when an executive walked by, pretending to swoon with ecstasy. To win arguments—and they were constantly bickering with what they called the "Bozo Sausage Factory"—they'd grab their breasts, point them at you, and advance on you like gunfighters. They'd tell you where to shove your ideas and show you how. Lunchtime was a rush to harass bikers and construction workers: "Will you look at that big pillow hanging over his gas tank! Are you pregnant honey? I wish I had tits like yours! —You kissin' at us big boy; hey let's do it right here. Come on you big dirty stud, drop those pants and make us happy right NOW!"

None of us was safe during Male Liberation Week: suddenly you'd be held by the gluteus maximus, or something even worse, while a lady smacked her lips and commented in detail to the whole City Room on what she was finding.

Lois hales from Cleveland, the youngest of seven kids in a well-to-do Catholic family on the Heights. She was excommunicated ("I'll swear it on any fucking Bible you like!") by a priest seeking to terrorize her from skipping Mass. "Man, that was great—I was *free* at eight years old!" Her older brothers and sisters teased and belittled her: her talent and brains made her a perfect target. But she was too strong, she claims, to suffer traumas like mine. "Shit, Clark, Cleveland was the Big City for rubes like you, but it was mighty small for me. I took my Fullbright and never looked back! Don't ever give me any crap about missing Kansas. When you grow up, you realize there never *were* any good old days."

"Something's funny here, Clark!"—again and again that yell, startling us from our urgent labors to Bring Today To You, heralds a classic of investigative journalism. My favorites include: "Cancer in Your Mattress," a series about toxicity in the new Stimuspleep Dermal Nocturnal Infusions sweeping the country; "The Red Meat Menace," about mass-killed herds smuggled by evil Latin cartels from 18.2 million toxic quarantined acres into fast- food product-lines; "Sex, Steroids, and the American Family," demonstrating the inverse relationships between athletic and sexual performance, and between muscle and genital size in males. Lois stunned

the Pentagon by citing top secret research establishing the "Negative Volumetric Erotic Curve." The killer article, "Holocaust in the Crotch," caused agonizing reappraisals and Chapter 11 filings by gymnasia across the land, after its graphic mid-body photos from classified Eyes-Only studies of armed service recruits blanketed the Internet and the media.

"Does America Really Care about our Breasts?" begins, "I am a breast. Let me tell you what you've done to me for three centuries."

"I'm feeling it, Clark!" signals a New Age interpretive classic. Lois injects her self, her true spirit into these. In my favorite she sits atop the Times Square Marriott Marquis Hotel rotating 360 degrees, savoring the cuisine and the wine cellar. Her spirit gathers itself for an omni-directional meditation, transforming Lois into a trans-temporal-and-sexual Walt Whitman, updating his visioning: South, she sees a stream of immigrants bringing us a cultural heritage more valuable than any product loaded or unloaded on our docks. East, she sees the exultant neon of Times Square surpassing its spiritual artistic ancestor, the stained glass of cathedrals of Mother Europe. West, she sees the vast continent, grasped and subdued by the religious enthusiasm of our forebears. North she sees and feels the Hudson and the Erie Canal, physical and spiritual connections to the Great Lakes, those vast ventricles gushing forth tangible and intangible sustenance from our heartland.

She asks me to do some digging into the Sling matter ("Better call in Supe Clark.") while she writes a verbal portrait of the "twin towers" of New Age Poetry, Robert Duckey and James Blahre. She fills me in on their stature and status before she heads south to do the interview.

Under pressure from WE, their major stakeholder, Duckey and Blahre agreed in principle recently to merge their poetry corporations. Duckey's penetration of the female market has peaked, and Blahre's appearances at the Promise Reapers tours pull fewer men. Rigorous application of MAMA management techniques to their enterprises have failed to jump-start the shares of Duckey Unlimited and Iron Sufficiency, Inc., listed o-t-c, which stagnate despite the perpetual bull market.

SEC filings by Golden Sacks reveal a cogent, synergistic, demographically -anchored marketing plan enabling these seminal figures to enhance their cross-gender penetration.

Golden achieves an investment banking first in its red herring for D&B Dynamically-Fused Enterprises: the deconstruction and marketability analysis of the classic Reapers affirmation-chant:

"I am BOOM"
"I feel BANG"
"I matter BOOM"
"I can hurt BANG
"I feel my pai-ain BOOM
"I am a man BANG
"A spirit BOOM
"A feeling spirit BANG
"I touch me BOOM
"I touch you BANG (*the patented group hug-wave commences*)
"I sense me BOOM
"I sense you BANG
"I bless my spirit BOOM
"I bless your spirit BANG
"My heart and my spirit are
"Tender as my go-o-nads BOOM
"I am a blessed blessed spirit BOOM
"You are a blessed blessed spirit BANG BANG
"BANG BOOM BOOM BOOM"
"I make a sacred promise BOOM now BOOM (*hands to hearts*)
"To always be-e worthy of me-e-e-e-e-EE BOOM
'BOOM BOOM BOOM BANG" (*hands thump chests in time to sacred tom-toms*)

Golden's detailed analysis calls for a refashioning of the gonadic lines to delineate and encompass the consumption-triggers of females. The investment bank throws its full might behind the project, the hallowed words "fully confident" assuring investors the two principals will complete this reconstruction successfully.

Golden research created a stunning and provocative revamp of the founders' images: Duckey's new "erect bald-pate" and Blahre's resplendent "flowing white-haired prophetic" senior status will unblock their visual acceptance, now frozen by makeup and cosmetic procedures in a ho-hum "influential mid-life"cliché. Now the poets project a refreshed eco-psychic dynamism into the Seniors Markets, which have blown by Mid-Teens in volume of entertainment-consumption, by looking like themselves.

Lois is excited to interview them hot off a 24-7 blitz of talk-show appearances featuring their "unvarnished veracity of the self" experience. They adorn the cover of *Self* fixing us powerfully with their new look.

Arriving at the Olde Glen Duckey estate in Virginia horse-country near Lignum at dusk, she admires the Duckey crest on the rising portcullis, filigreed guitars addressing each other a la duello above the motto "Semper Ipse." The door-chime plays the theme from the *Male Delivery I-IX* movie-epics in two-part harmony. Thick ironwood portals swing open at the anthem's climax, and Lois follows a blood-red plush carpet through a cavernous peaked hall bristling from floor to eaves with armor, antlers, pikes, hides, head, maces, shark jaws, stuffed fish, gun racks, flyfishing rods, Gatling guns, elephant tusks, palisadoes, halibut hooks, cannonballs, wolf jaws, catapults, model Humvees, classic jet-skis, model Range Rovers, stuffed raptors, model Apache attack 'copters, autographed Big Bertha drivers, cannonballs, and an authentic guillotine—all collected from sets of the classics of 20th-century cinema by Steven Zauberberg, F. Ford Copula, and Elia Cossack. Torchlights throw the collection into menacing relief, enhanced by red bulbs in the eye-sockets and teeth of the trophies.

The vast mahogany doors of the anterior portal open tunefully when Lois crosses the sensors between a dolphin and a manatee. She squints to make out the famous men, silhouetted and backlit by a head-high gas fire at the nether end of the Duckey study. Heatwaves rise from the figures, as from asphalt in a desert. Duckey wears cowboy duds, Blahre a voluminous serape, matching in breadth his partner's legendary height.

Duckey takes Lois's hand and forearm into his vast hands. His gentle touch finds pressure points as, with relaxed grip, his fingers glide from the crook of her forearm to the fleshy webs between her fingers. Reminded of her natural skin therapy sessions on Park Avenue South, in which an octopus tentacle is applied to dry problem spots, Lois marvels at the poet's command of naturopathy. Blahre kisses her left hand, hiking his serape over his shoulder, and traces a balletic pirouette in the air with his free arm as he bows to her.

Feeling goosebumps on her arms, Lois chooses a straight-backed chair from the Cluny monastery, and whips out her notebook. A naggingly-familiar cloying odor suffuses the room. Duckey lowers himself into his beloved antelope-skin settee, shin, boot and spur swinging over the side. Blahre stands, right knee forward and flexed, poised to perform a gymnastic lunge.

Shit, I don't know why, but I'm scared of these dudes; something's funny and fucked. This is supposed to be a fun New-Ager. I'd better drop something on them.

"Why would men cloaked in spirit, men of such inspiring vision, allow layoffs in your firms?"

"Them's just rumors little lady. Where'd you hear that."

An edge in Duckey's voice belies his Southern graces.

Lois quotes "Heard on the Street" and reads from Golden's red herring.

Blahre straightens, arms akimbo beneath his serape.

Duckey's clothes gather; his boots clank and his spurs ring as he bolts from his chair—"Skee-use me lettle lay-dee—" and bends low to whisper past Blahre's famous flowing locks, tinged with yellow and blue from their middle period.

"Yes oh yes!" Blahre exclaims.

Duckey's graces intensify.

"Ain' et a cryin' shame honey we hayve to tyalk 'bout 'ese ch'ere naysty things; less us break this off fur whah yee-ew really come here. Less us cut this sweet lay-dee in on the fahnest tracks from our nee-ew books, eh Jim."

"Ah yes, Bob, ah yes yes, if she'll only allow," and he pauses to watch his right hand perform the famous circle-gesture before them.

Duckey stands on his desk and declaims down to Lois, accompanying himself on a guitar amped through his wa-wa pedal. Blahre fills the intervals with wistful images inducing dreamy meditation. Lois struggles to take on Duckey's rhythmic verbal assault, struggles to register the deep, metaverbal tropes Blahre completes with his wrist and fingers, conducting a chamber orchestra of the echoic spirit. She wrestles with the masculinity; she pursues the elusive spirituality, struggling so hard to comprehend this charged moment that her consciousness travels to the brink of dissolution. She knows this is a great moment vouchsafed to her because of...*because of what?* she wonders as she fights to stay awake and Duckey fades to a huge echo, Blahr to a distant breeze and the warmth of the fire and the mysterious but familiar odor is a blanket on her mind and she stretches herself to stay with it all until she feels her wrists held behind her head, her long full skirt over her face, her knees pushed back and apart. . .and rage impels her to writhe and scream, "LET ME GO, YOU GREASY PIGFUCKERS!"

But I am there! I crash through the portal, splintering it, silencing its duel forever. The shock-waves shake loose the armory and the trophies as I lock onto the poets menacing Lois, sweep them away from my shrieking, kicking friend, and pinion them to iron spikes atop the vast mantelpiece. Duckey's dungarees hang from his boots; Blarhe struggles to gather his serape about his lank little body.

Lois is still. Her little pink dimples are gone. The flesh is drawn in towards her teeth.

"I'm here, Lois. You're safe. Are you o.k.? You look like you've seen a ghost."

Her brown eyes pop open. I'm so relieved. They open wider, take me in, take in the fire, fix on the villains above it. She grins.

"Shit, Supe, why'd you take so long? —Hey, lift me, I'm gonna twist off those pigfuckers' ugly nuts."

I chuckle.

"Lois, I believe a court of law will isolate them from innocent women for a long, long time."

"Court of law? These fuckin' old boys'll get away with a slap on the wrist. Shit, they'll hire Johnny Cochrane and try *me*."

Duckey piped up.

"Ah thank yuh've git us hwrong, Miz Lane an' Syoop.— Ah's three-illed to meetcha, syur. —Weez jes' doon Mr. Blee-aah's totem scrotum ritchool, thasall."

"Some fuckin' totem. See what I mean Supe?"

"Let me handle this, Lois."

I fly up and unhook the villains. I place them, shaking, knees pressed together facing the blaze. I am careful to hide their genitals from Lois. I order them to put their clothes in shape.

"Now Mr. Duckey, Mr. Blahre, you look a little faint. Let me tone you up."

I grasp them by the scruffs of their necks and give them a good shaking. Duckey's flesh washes across his skeleton, across his jaw. He looks like a jug pouring into his boots. Blahre squeaks; his arms and legs fly loose like semaphores

"Now, gentlemen. I believe you owe the lady an apology."

Silence. I fly along walls of the great entrance, smashing the memorabilia.

Duckey bellows: "That collection's insured for a hundred mill!'

I grab him, shake him again, enduring the wicked odor of liquor-breath, his body, his gas. I set him down closer to the fire. The whole place smells repugnantly odd.

Lois grins, "Shit, Supe, you are you trying to work a beat with me?"

Blahre, who has watched me in a posed attitude of fear and awe, animates himself. He begins talking, as if in a trance, a groan and drone I dismiss at first as poetic stuff, until I pick out the words, "young Rickey."

...Mmmm oh sweet lord it was an experience; the inside was positively soft and lined with neon filigree flashing rendering the exterior void more void-like, and in New York how can that be? And I realize that our driver, a simply magnificent black man is experiencing his own reality, for he is driving us into these dark outer regions called boroughs, and he is wearing impenetrable shades, creating an inner and outer black-on-black. Contemplating his serene negritude, I relaxed, feeling his command of the large but responsive product of Bavarian precision, and let go, for truly we were "dropping our days" and traversing in our soft warm cocoon "the harping altar of the fury's fateful fusion."

Young Rickey rode shotgun, as he deliciously phrased it, knowledgeably complimenting our driver on his choice of soul tracks, and setting the amazing scene for us through the clever mike from behind bulletproof glass:

"Yes, leaving Brooklyn Bridge we enter a true heart of darkness, and we are exploring like Ponce de Leon to bring the alchemy of the market's invisible hand to this space, and we shall return transfixed, refreshed, and future-fitted. Gentlemen, please unsheathe your goggles, but do NOT don them before my signal—for you will risk permanent disorientation should you do so before it is truly dark."

We unzipped ballistic-material bags monogrammed RH to discover military night vision goggles.

"Yes, gentlemen, the latest hardware from the frontiers of guerrilla combat. We have word the next war will be in the desert, and I want you men of spirit to experience combat in the wild dark reaches."

Then flickering darkness, relieved by the sounds of soul. I remember a memorial arch, and the Allegorical Figure of Brooklyn, before a too too marmoreal edifice, and then as we rode a gentle incline to something called the Interborough, Rickey announced with oh such meaningful portent, "Gentlemen, don the goggles—" and my life changed.

I see a wilderness of litter. A chaos. I see ginkgo-weeds whose leaves are hardened bits of gray paper. I see rats swarming over the plastic packages of half-eaten junk food, rats swarming like furry rivers gushing along the embankment. I see derelicts picking over torn and stained clothing, and boxes and boxes end-to-end in intricate patterns like dun dominoes domiciling the derelicts. And so many fires! Oh, the fires illuminating hideously diseased Hogarthian faces hunched to their toxic warmth, crunching and spitting bits of dead animals roasted on spindly spits.

And oh the beatings, and the thefts, and the rapes—and Rick was in front going "Hey, wow, dig that, guys, this beats Ultimate Combat!" Bob pulled steadily on his hip flask muttering "shee-it."— Oh oohh *it was worse than Dickensian, worse even than Zola-esque.*

And we slow down, and I'm thinking oh god no what can our driver be doing. Is he releasing us like prey to his brethren—when I see a monumental electric fence protecting mountainous heaps of electrified scrap-metal, and sparks are arcing from them, dead and dying derelicts twitching or still at their feet, a lone stunned derelict crawling in circles like an experimental rat, and I see dark men in arc-welding helmets and men with gigantic laser-saws, and beyond I see a line of shiny cars. A hellish deja vue, for it almost looks like the entrance, black-lit, to the drive-in theaters of my dear provincial youth, a long line of rough-teen-age louts in upscale vehicles— Range Ravagers, Land Bruisers, Implodas, Humpers, F111Primes, Kennedys, Cosmics— to what looks like a ticket-kiosk. But lo! They receive neat piles of new bills, leaving their cars and swaggering into the night. Rickey rushes excitedly to the kiosk, speaks animatedly to a being attached to the hands dispensing cash, pats a Ravager on its flank.

As Bob snores, I push away his limp bulk, and I struggle to digest the myriad of sensations gripping me. I am experiencing the eschaton, trapped in a portentous dystopia, until the warm consciousness suffuses my being, this is the beginning, the inception, the incarnation, *as Rickey has prophesied, and I am at its fiery crucible.*

The air-tight door to the limo clasps shut. With his self-confident grin, Rickey leans toward us. "Gentlemen, you must keep this to yourselves. This is classified. This, gentlemen, is economic alchemy, it is the incarnation of All-Source Eco-Capital…"

"A fucking chop-shop. I knew that little prick Rick was screwing around with the wiseguys. Assholes like him love mob chic. But I wonder why he's doing this shit. — What else can you tell us, boys?"

But Duckey nudges Blahre, who goes silent. Lois grabs a wolf's jaw. She growls and menaces the poets' groins with the bared fangs.

"Woof-woof, little boys. Ever hear of a shredded-ball barbecue? What are you and Rick doing? Maybe I'll ask my pal Supe to be nice to you—OR MAYBE NOT YOU COCKSUCKERS, NOW TALK."

I restrain her.

"Now, now Lois. Let's let the might and majesty of the Law take its course."

"Bullshit Supe, something's funny and fucked here. You're a swell dude, but sometimes I think you're as naive as Clark. You think a cracker jury is going to convict these famous hot shits for attempting to sleep-rape an uppity northern bitch with poetry? I think these guys can give up Rick. The little ugly prick loved to go backstage with their groupies, and fly them all around in his corporate jet. I think this is connected to Sally blowing Bryan."

"Now, now little lady. We're talking about a senior executive at WE."

"Senior asshole. He's never made us a cent. All he does is give me the once-over. All these born again hypocrites are horny. Listen, Supe, you never bust anything open unless you follow your gut.

"—And you know what that smell is? It's SemenEssence by Klein."

But I refuse to allow Lois to get carried away. I cannot believe that Rick Hussell, senior executive, son of Mayor Hussell, business partner and protégé of Senator T'Omato, can be anything other than an upstanding citizen. We turn

the scoundrels in to the local sheriff, who is amazed and thrilled that I am operating in his jurisdiction. A plaque by jail entrance beside the Confederate colors says Jefferson Davis slept there when it was a humble country inn. I consent to do my standard, non-classified display of powers for the sheriff, the deputies, and the friendly inmate sleeping off a bender. They get a particular thrill when I count the money in their pants pockets. I autograph the hole I burn into his old oak desk, next to Stonewall Jackson's authentic carved initials.
I vow to return to testify against the malefactors.

"Let's get home, little lady, and leave these imaginary plots behind."

SHARPIE ATTACK
ALERT
"HOW TO PIN DOWN A POLITICIAN"
WE'LL HAVE THE LATEST, PLUS THE WEATHER.
NEWS
THE
MURD
TEAM
ATTACK
!!!!

Rick's dad, Mayor Herbert Hussell, is the most-revered New York politician since Mayor LaGuardia. A dominant Irishman reminiscent of the glory days of Walker and O'Dwyer, he emerged from his quiet calculations as State Comptroller during Mayor Giusillini's second term to save that emblem of indomitable order and justic from the weaknesses of his strengths, and to assure Guisillini's ascent to the corridors of economic might.

Few citizens realize that Rudolph Giusillini's future lay in the balance during the spring of 2000; I have pieced together this account from police files, suppressed news footage, and from conversations with Lois.

On that fateful day Giusillini was leading the event closest to his heart, the Italian-American Anti-Defamation League Men's Sensitivity March, an event he had purged of its sordid and bloody creation by the Genovese family, endowing it with the psychic purity and healing balms of the New Age. Following rallies in Columbus Circle addressed by the Cardinal, by Italian entrepreneurs and athletes, and by Buddhist celebrities, the marchers proceeded East to the Queensboro Bridge, at the foot of which they were joined by the Proud Italian Mother's March, bussed up from Mulberry Street. Mothers and men: these heartwarming celebrations of ethnicity and gender were renowned for the fragrant, colorful pushcarts from which the cheery mothers distributed rich delicacies to the hungry men, and to the deep crowds lingering the avenues, delicacies exhausted year after year as soon as the march reached 96th Street. Television coverage featured interviews with strong men weeping over their mothers, wives, and children.

But the Reverend Al Sharpie hated these marches: erroneously, the African-American community believed that the route, marching through the old Italian community in East Harlem to a phalanx of police vans, limos, and buses closing 125th Street from Frederick Douglass Boulevard to the Triboro Bridge, had been chosen to provoke people of color and anger community leaders like Sharpie. And so in the watershed political year 2000 Sharpie planned a black community rally along the route, vowing to be peaceful, but outspoken.

Sharpie rallied his followers to a vacant lot just above the Metropolitan Hospital Center, cleared forty years earlier to make way for a daycare facility. Politicians chose this venue regularly as a backdrop illustrating a rich array of messages: economic justice; gun, crime, drug and self control; racial justice; urban and moral renewal through family and religious values. Elevating their thumbs, making victory signs with their fingers or fists, they aimed their promises at the rotting bullet-pocked buildings bordering it. Neo-Hypo-Realistic film-makers from the Brooklyn Zauberberg-de Nero lots released rats, roaches, pit bulls, one-eyed tomcats, skateboards, prostitutes, BMX bikes, and juvenile drug-dealers across its sordid surface. Nevertheless, over the decades no reporter besides Murray Kempton discerned any change in the lot or the buildings. Kempton noted that a door had been painted.

Reverend Sharpie prepared his community for the onslaught by rallying a crowd of children and derelicts for three hours with his oratory and his church rock choir. Alerted to the March's approach by the roar of Tactical Police helicopters, he rechanneled and rekindled his oratorical flow. Throwing back his shining hair to confront lower Manhattan, arms across his deep chest, he shouted, "MY PEOPLE OF HARLEM, BROTHERS, SISTERS, *DO YOU SEE WHAT I SEE*? (The kids nodded. A derelict growled, 'Fuck them dago crackers.')

"Now be cool, brothers and sisters, be cool. We're gonna show them a warm welcome, and we're gonna let the TRUTH ROLL OVER THEM LIKE MIGHTY WATERS! (*'PISS ON THE FUCKIN GREASEBALLS!'*) And brother I feel your pain and your black rage, but I want you to remember the little children and the cameras (*'Sorry little darlings; you be so cute; I'll never, ever, do it again; never ever, I swear on my sweet momma's grave, honey, I do swear…'*) *OK BROTHER*, and I want you to know I KNOW, the MAN Al Sharpie knows, there's a time to

CONFRONT (*'no shit, brother'*), and you know I know how to CONFRONT THEM ALL like the MAN I am (*'Where'd you get that hair?'*), and there's a time to DEAL, yes, they think we're too dumb to DEAL, but we're not STUPID, brothers and sisters like they think, we know how to DEAL, yes we do, and that's what we're gonna DO, brothers and sisters, because we're smarter than that phony bad-ass Rudy. He thinks he's *bad*? You think that little skinny-ass politician is *bad*? I tell you he isn't. (*'You ain't shittin me; dago cracker took my methadone, the motherfucker. —I'M sorry, little darlin.'*)

"It may be FATAL for a brother to take a peaceful walk in THAT ITALIAN BENSONHURST but a whole LOUD PROVOCATIVE group of Italians can march safely in my Harlem because AL SHARPIE IS SMART, AND YOU'RE ALL BEHIND ME. (Sweeping his arms across the lot. *'Hey, Al, get on the tube with that sister with the* tits, *man.'*).

"OK, OK brothers and sisters, here he is...Now you-all watch me show Rudy some stuff."

Reverend Sharpie broke into huge grin. From the height of his platform he spread his arms wide as if to bless the approaching paraders, who numbered twenty-four men, forty-three women and seventy-six reporters by now, and, assured that the cameras were ready, he called out,

"Welcome to my Harlem, Rudy. Sorry your march is so small. We're here to greet you in peace. —And *will you look there at that bee-eautiful sweet Momma*? (as he saw the cameras focus on a marcher in a floral dress just behind the Mayor and Hussell). Is that your momma, Rudy?"

There was silence, and the Mayor running at the stage, jumping up the steps, the Reverend Sharpie's eyes widening and a river of sweat glistening on his face. The Mayor landed a right cross to the man of God's head; sweat sprayed, and his facial flesh flowed like wakes ejected from a deep-hulled craft, stretching to its tensile limit inches beyond his cheekbone and his bared teeth, as he absorbed a roundhouse left uppercut to his belly. These classic blows failed to derange the senses of the Reverend, who, emitting a rending blast blending a roar a moo a grunt and a snort, enfolded the Mayor, wrathfully risking infighting with his vast moist antagonist, in an engrossing bear hug. Just as, too late to intervene, you see with pangs of heart a doughty ant trammeled in the web of the death-dealing spider, so you saw the sinewy arms and legs of the metropolis's plucky leader flailing and twitching, his slight torso mired in the moist hug.

Ceaselessly roaring Sharpie slammed the Mayor to the stage with a thunderous torso-drop, and moaning he lay atop the prostrate politician, heaving great gulps of air into his liquid pectorals, sobbing, and hissing into the ear exposed by the mayor's close-cropped locks, "Why'd you fuck up our scene, motherfucker, why? We had a good thing going, you little prick. All the media in the world are here, man."

Giusillini's flailing weakened, slowed, stopped. But the awed, frozen spectators realized he had but recruited his aura and his grit, inspired by the Columbus Circle rituals, for with one mighty effort he broke an arm free, and grabbed Sharpie's hair, the lengths of which however slid through his grasp, while, gagging on the river of perspiration mingled with hairy unguents, he clamped the Reverend's outer dewlaps between his foreteeth in a mighty chomp. The Reverend split the air with a renewed medley of martial ejaculations, and had lifted his meaty leg to administer the coup de grace, a knee to the civic groin, when a blue vanguard of New York's Finest, blazoned by chroniclers of metropolitan strife as "the soul cops" for their bringing normal levels of police practice to Harlem, smothered the action.

Seeing which, Herb Hussell took command. Slim digital phone to left ear, he shoved pale and wan Guisillini into an inky limo that bulled in from a side street. The mayor was mumbling, "That nigger can't touch my mother." Hussell worked the media troops, warning them not to incite a long hot summer, reminding them of his tightness with Rupert Murd. He huddled with Reverend Sharpie, who nodded and smiled frequently. Finally he strode to the station house to meet with the captain of the Soul Patrols.

And so the fight, according to the *World* and all responsible media, never happened.

Lois Lane traveled to Harlem, interviewed seventeen adult eyewitnesses from the neighborhood, checked her facts with police sources, and wrote the true story. It was never printed: Brian O'Brien reminded her that a story based on the consistent testimony of black eyewitnesses was, in the *Daily World*, unsubstantiated and uncorroborated. She was called before the CSC.

A popular late-night comedian did a routine called "How to Pin Down a Politician," contrasting the Sharpie wrestling style with Hulk Hogan's, using bootleg videotapes in slow motion to diagram the action like a sportscaster. He disappeared from the air for a month, and *Variety* detailed his sufferings from a medley of health problems.

The Reverend Al Sharpie's career flourished: The Sharpie Foundation to Save Humanity was erected on the northern half of the vacant lot. His career as a Christian gangsta rapper took of in the unimproved half, thanks to brutally realistic Grammy-Winning Zauberberg-de Nero videos, financed by the Madonna Foundation, showing Sharpie rhythmically redeeming the squalor of his people.

Herb Hussell's power in New York City, Long Island, and upstate was unchallenged thenceforth. Privately Governor Attaki defers to this man of quiet strength.

Hussell has mastered the art of the sound byte. His bland, scultpted words resonate in all media, and illustrate a healthy range of social and political viewpoints.

"If you want to be President, come talk to us in New York."

Hussell's pithy advice to aspirants for the highest office resonate through the three-year presidential primary season. State leaders from both parties vied to hold position their contests as the front-runner, the decisive event, moving them earlier in bold three-month and six-month intervals until they closed in on the Innauguration. But the canny Hussell blunted these moves with this broad hint that his financial and media resources would be forever beyond the reach of any presidential contender who failed to contest the New York primaries which never budged from their date just before the conventions. Even triumphant front-runners wage all-out campaign warfare here, channeling oceans of leveraged PAC wealth into WE media to attack the offshore and domestic evils and enemies they will eradicate when elected.

"We want to know who's asking us for something," explains Hussell.

Voter turnout is at 99% in New York, spurred by prize coupons, discounted Lotto subscriptions, samples from product rollouts, and media stars working the precincts and polling-places. Hussell expedited the exercise of our franchise by assigning each citizen a bar code. He dismissed with a grunt and a chuckle Lois' questions about privacy. But Lois persisted, and there was silence on City Hall's steps as he leveled his stony stare on her, cleared his throat with his signature admonitory roar, and after pausing for a full ten-count, replied simply, "Lois honey, this city has been in business 375 years, this state 223, and this country 225. Are you accusing me of meddling with success like that? —Next question."

7 DEVELOPING BEDFORD-STUYVESANT FOR THE FUTURE

Hope came to Bedford-Stuyvesant in the mid 1960's, when Bobby Kennedy walked the grimy streets of that poor neighborhood in his shirtsleeves, riding tides of thrilled adulation and blessing those people with a positive message of uplift and faith in the future. Bobbie and his retinue of journalists, intellectuals and athletes understood the importance of self-improvement, and challenged the throngs to believe in themselves. Churches in Bed-Stuy got out the vote for him, as they had for Nelson Rockefeller, who also walked among the people, touching them, suffering their touch, and building faith in his promises.

Now the promises are fulfilled: Rupert Murd is on the scene, armed with proprietary analyses demonstrating that Bed-Stuy, responding to the fiscal stimulation his lobbyists delivered from City Hall and Albany, has achieved the coveted milestone: it has risen from Emerging Market to Pre-Conditional status! Franklin Avenue has been rechristened the Avenue of the Future, and a Magic Johnson Entertainment Mall Complex will renew the entire neighborhood east of Fulton Street bounded by Franklin, Lafayette, and Marcy Avenues. This plot, formerly containing small shops, a Carnegie public library and outmoded housing from the 19th and early-20th centuries, made paltry contributions to the tax base. Its antiquated subway impeded the trickle of automobiles venturing into so backward a zone. The once-fine houses generations had divided into a myriad of units, the back yards in which residents tended fruit trees, vegetables, carrier pigeons, the small alleys that connect the backyards, often dating to the days of horsedrawn vehicles and grazing livestock—these underbuilt volumes were perfect sites for parking lots. Whole rows of brick and brownstone homes have been bulldozed, loaded into hoppers, hoisted, and carted in away in under an hour to recycling sites along the Gowanus Canal and the Newtown Creek, where the usable brick and stone is powerwashed and resold to developers in Westchester and Nassau counties, satisfying the suburban rage for the natural distressed look in decks, patios and retaining walls.

Lois has written insightfully that these rebuilds start with Magic and end with Starbucks, and she's right: at the inception of the process, street-interview specialists extract for WE Marketing intelligence on the hottest clothing looks and the coolest music sounds among the people of the ghetto. Module I of the Mall presents these trendy goods in a profusion beyond the wildest dreams of the shopping-starved denizens. Module I reaches out close and personal, bringing in the hottest stars of high-impact entertainment for the month-long openings. They wear the new looks, sign CDs, draw symbols on torn T-shirts, sign spaces on flesh between tattoos, and mingle enthusiastically with their adoring consumers to the extent their armed bodyguards permit.

The New York Knickerbockers were there, Al Sharpie was there rapping, along with Brooklyn residents Hot Stick Blood Cash Smash and Spike Lee to smother any sympathy for a few ancient toothless preservationists and tree-huggers perpetrating a feeble protest against development. Spike captured the moment proudly, "Some white folks think we're not *ready* to have what they have in the 'burbs, do you believe it? Lets show them, bothers and sisters: our 'hoods are just as good as theirs; we *are* ready to be an economic force like them—our green's as green as their green, and our plastic works just as good, don't it! Some local nuts think they own the 'hood, do you believe it? *Nobody* but you and me owns it, brothers and sisters—I grew up here and I'm proud of us all! And let it go forth, and you're the first to hear it, friends: the opening ceremony for my next film, 'Booker in Bed' will be right here at this cineplex, where its roots live!"

This high-touch entertainment fuels enthusiastic consumption of high-turnover apparel, accessories, music and fast food. The Magic J MegaPlex features the latest cinema-releases, whose calibrated-impact sex and graduated-intensity violence draw all demographics. The imported stars fondle the objects, munch the foods and model the clothing they are premiering in the movies. The early cash-flow infallibly allows Global Entertainment to retire the short-term paper it issues to cover costs during the hectic run-up to the Opening.

My mission today: to help the cream of civic leadership and society dedicate the WE Foundation's donation to the neighborhood, a lovely vest-pocket park, featuring 45,000 square feet of sparkly concrete adorned with the latest recreation experiences from Disney and Dreamworks—scaled-down replicas of the recreation experiences in the fast-food outlets in the new MJEMC. My cue is Giusillini's pause after proclaiming, "...and we have wrestled these mean streets from the animals preying upon the law-abiding, church-going citizens of Bedford-Stuyvesant!"

I drop with a "whoooosh" next to Rudy, the governor, the mayor, Heraldo Riviera and the other leading luminaries from business, the charity circuit and the arts who exclaim "oooooohhh, look kids. Can you believe it?" Like Santa Claus, I delight and awe youngsters. Today there are five rows of them, scrubbed up in their Sunday bests. The cameras catch their innocent eyes widening in surprise, fear, joy at my vertical drop: Brooklyn has never seen me in action. Their parents in the next five rows, sweating but joyous in their brightly-colored church finery, burst into rhythmic screams and songs of praise.

I sense interference: a sickly little girl bursts into tears. Her Mom and Dad growl at her from behind. Her Dad makes a fist, points to his belt buckle. But her sobs outlast the joyful commotion. Rudy chuckles, pauses to give the technicians in the trailer time to split the screen. "It's all right, little darling. Supe's your big brother. He's our Gotham good guy, here to keep you safe and make you happy." The charitable luminaries applaud, "Oh how cute how sweet look at those big eyes! Isn't it a shame they have to grow up?"

I whisper to Rudy. He nods,"—What's your name honey, don't be shy. Tell us all your name, cutie."

The little girl mumbles at the microphones in her face. "How's that? Ah uh T Y E S H A, my how lovely, a cute little African name, honey, almost as pretty as you are.

"Let me ask you, Tyesha, would you like to be the first kid *ever* to use all these wonderful authentic Dreamworks and

Disney play experiences? Won't your folks be proud of their little girl? —Supe, *will* you?"

I fly down to little Tyesha, land at her scuffed unmatching shoes. The knobs of her kneecaps bulge from the meatless bones of her legs. She stares up at me, shivering, new tears streaking the salt from the old tears on her dull ashy cheeks. She's the only little girl with no ribbons in her corn rows, and her scalp is mottled with scabs. Her shoulders stoop, wrinkling the faded cotton dress too small even for her bony frame. She has scratches on her neck, and round scars line her stick-like arms.

I whisper in her ear, pushing the mikes away from our mouths, "Tyesha, you *will* be the very first of all the kids on any play-experience you choose. Let's you and me take our own special ride first, so you can calm down, o.k. honey?"

She gives the slightest nod, glancing back at her parents. She whites of her eyes are dust-colored, and they are bloodshot. I've never known a child like this. The kids in Manhattan, Westchester and the Island rush at me, touch and grab me, demanding rides and autographs. Tyesha raises her skinny arms. I lift her and she buries her head under my chin. She emits a disturbing odor, but I stifle my disgust. She hugs my neck as we rise. I hope she can see the upraised faces, the kids wishing they were where she is. She's a limp bundle of skin and bones.

"Are you exited, honey?"

No answer.

"Are you all right darling?"

A faint, "Yeah."

"I'll bet you never had a day like this!"

She's quiet.

"Have you ever had such fun?"

"No."

"Are you ready to be thrilled by the new play-experiences?"

No answer. She holds tighter, buries her head deeper.

"Honey, we've *got* to play. Let's take the first ride together. You can sit on my lap. OK?"

A slight nod.

We land on the top of the Singing Matterhorn.

"Isn't that wonderful, Tyesha? The beautiful music starts as soon as we're near. Did you see that lovely movie?"

She's quiet. She clings to my neck.

"Heeere we go, Tyesha!"

She is trembling when we're down, clinging and hiding her head under my chin.

"What's the matter, honey? Didn't you love that ride through the virtual Alps? Didn't you just love those little white virtual lambs?"

All I can see is her dirty dress and her little legs curled against my chest. She's like a bunch of sticks. I've never known a kid like this. She has no warmth, spark, spontaneity. I want to do something, anything for her, but I don't know what.

The former Mayor's speech goes on; he's getting impatient. He wants all the kids on the experiential experiences; he wants the crowd happy, and he needs to leave. The Building Bed-Stuy for the Future Ball is tonight, he needs to put in some quality work in the limo and his bunker in the World Financial Center.

"Look, look folks, our own Supe is taking little Tyesha down the "Singing Matterhorn. 'Do-oe, a deer, a fe-eemale deer.' Heh-heh heh-heh. You know what a bad singer I am folks, but I just get carried away. What a ride! What a lucky girl; the very first ever to use this newest-model experiential experience, and she does it thanks to Superman! Yes, folks, that's what we're all about: going the extra mile, the extra height even, heh-heh, to give you everything you need.

"AND NOW, on behalf of our kind sponsors Disney and Dreamworks—just hold back few more moments, kiddies—and on behalf of the co-chairs of our fund-raising committee, Nirvana Von Umph, Choo-Choo de Razzawall, Faustina Ochs-Bullsburger, and Claus von Bulow, who worked tirelessly behind the scenes to raise money to make this opening and tonight's ball possible—I declare the wonderful new play-experience open for the children of Bedford Stuyvesant! And parents, don't forget to take your little darlings across to the Magic Johnson Mall for shopping, fun entertainment and refreshments when you're done. Enjoy! God love and bless you all!"

Tyesha's parents are waiting for her as the other youngsters rush to play. They're angry. There's something restless about them. Each grabs an arm; the three walk away without a word, ignoring my pleasantries. Tyesha stares back at my feet, but her father yanks her away.

I always get through to kids This little girl baffles me. Her parents disturb me. I shall visit her as soon as possible. I want to hear their issues get to the bottom of whatever is bothering them.

click
click

8 MY NEW SIDEKICK

Today I'll straighten out this kid who's been harassing me on the Internet. He's holed up in Sunset Park, another area of the City new to me. He's a clever hacker—too smart for his own good. He calls himself IT, the Cyber-Terrestrial. I don't like his attitude.

Sunset Park looks like row after row of matchboxes on end, faded fiberboard or aluminum siding covering the original brick and brownstone. I checked it out: it was a typical neighborhood, a village within the City, until Moses ran the Gowanus Parkway over it. Unready for this leap into progress, the residents continued their pedestrian ways, baffled by the dark noisy overpass splitting them apart. Soon families wending their way to church, the sons polished and starched into dignity, the daughters in frills like walking bakery cakes, were stunned and abashed to encounter prostitutes lining their sidewalks to service the truckers whose gigantic rigs added obstruction and danger to their simple lives.

And because the residents and the small shopkeepers were unable to adapt to the progress wrought by roads and trucks servicing efficient new shopping-units like supermarkets, they permitted urban decay to afflict their children: gangs formed, drugs circulated, schools rotted, and poverty infected them all, along with new ethnic groups that had little sense of clean European village traditions. And so another blighted area, which responsible citizens could do no more than motor over, defaced an outer borough.

The kid's apartment is the top floor of a faded green building. The concession stand on the corner sells ice in colorful multi-flavors. Children fail to realize that the magic of those colors and flavors is created by carcinogens. Idle hot dog, pretzel, and roasted-chestnut pushcarts from Manhattan are parked on the street. I never realized where they came from.

I arrive without warning through the roof hatchcover.

The place is a shocking mess; it smells like sugar and ashtrays.

"Hey, why'd you wait so long to get here, Supe, I've been trying to get you here for fuckin' ages, you know."

He's glued to his powerful docked laptop; no eye contact as he speaks and puffs on a cigarette. Customized systems crowd a big table before a dirty streaked window looking down and out at the harbor. I see Lady Liberty past the dead bugs attracted by the light he burns at all hours. Subterranean water and detritus provide moist nooks and wet vacancies for mosquito-breeding. I make a mental note to call in the chemical bombers.

"Clark Kent informed me you'd sent him some obscene messages. You've got lots of questions to answer, young man."

"Cut the crap. You're Kent. It takes two seconds to figure that. OK? Hey, I've been trying to get through to you to warn you what's going down."

"You may think you have important information, but obscenity and insults cannot be justified as means."

"Look, it's what you do. It got you here."

"Just who do you think you are, young man?"

"Me? I'm James Riegelstein. Everybody calls me JR—you've probably heard of my so-called business scandal: bunch of so-called grownups who couldn't get off their asses and do their jobs—just like you, Supe.

"God, I used to think you were so cool: you had the edge, man. But you're just a sellout and a stooge."

I pick him up, plant him on his feet, look him sternly in the eye. He can't stand still, scratching all over, shifting from one foot to another, pulling his pants from his anus. He wears a torn sweater with a check pattern. He smells of tobacco. He reaches for a cigarette; I snatch the pack away.

"Yeah, yeah get rough with me. But what're you going to do when you and Lane are fired from *The World*? Shit, Supe, get real."

"If you have information, James, let's hear it. But I want no obscene remarks, particularly about the lady."

"OK, OK, I don't blame you. She's a babe compared to that Cherry witch who's dancing circles around you. —Look, if you'd gotten out here sooner, I could have told you what those poet pricks would try on Lane..."

"That's not public, how do you know that, James?"

"Yeah, yeah, protect the innocent. Worry about who knows what, not about what's going down.

"—OK, see those antennae out there, and this equipment: I can get into any corporate system I want, monitor any phone I want, email any goddamn bigwig I feel like talking to. I'm sitting here in goddamn Brooklyn knowing more than you ever dreamed of knowing, Supe. I figure I can get some shit done, I can line up the big guys. So I get Bill Grates and Paul Gallons on email. I tell them they have the bucks to fix the whole Washington school system instead of ripping off taxpayers to build ballparks where some faggot in tight pants waves a club because his dick is falling off from steroids or some unevolved apes in pads smash each other to bits—I told them they could fix things up for kids, and they could stake the government assholes to save every tree, owl, and wetspot in the West. So Grates answers me personally when he sees his IT weenies can't shut me out and he explains how his foundation is "empowering and facilitating" the trickle-down effect of his "public trust" and sends me a proposal form. Gallons just threatens to prosecute me to the full extent, big deal."

"Young man, you're not giving me any information I can use."

"OK, OK I thought we could really talk, Supe. You were my hero. I get lonely out here. When I dropped out my folks noticed I was gone after a few days, notified the so-called authorities, and went back to yelling and beating on each other in front of the tube.

"Yeah, and I wanted to be the new you, IT the Cyberhero. I tried little boy scout stuff like you. I rescued those noisy old biddies who disappeared when Mr. Bast's house got developed. I tracked them down to where they were jammed up in the King County flight deck—that's a fuckin' hole. They sat there scared shitless with their good posture and shit, shivering in the middle of the loonies drooling and screaming and flopping on the crappy floor, and I get them a nice garden apartment in Park Slope and let it out to the neighbor yuppies and bobos they're decayed noble stuff. Now they have soirees and shit.

"But o.k., Supe, let's get down. Kent and Lane are in deep shit.

"Lane's going to get fired first. Rick Hussell has blown it: the little dork hangs out with the wiseguys because of their so-called glamour, they scam him into using their scrap metals in MAMA. You and Lane are getting near this because those poet pricks open their mouths: little Rickey loves their so-called masculine auras and he diddles their groupies. You and Lane don't understand shit. Rick's little toy lab the CSC monitors everything you do, say, write (*I'm thinking about this journal, and how I can protect Lois from Rick…*) Yeah, they know what's in your so-called book; shit, Supe, Cherry Trinken personally tutored the ugly little prick in sex and keeps him fixed up. They know they'll never run WE, that'll be Murd's son who turns newspapers into tabloids or his slant squeeze, so Cherry and Rick work together to protect their turf.

"Rick's trying to cover his ass by getting Lane fixed, but the little prick is worried Sal might come after him too so he's holed up in that pukey Irish family compound letting Momma feed him hag and shit."

I am enduring a sudden pounding migraine but I am seeing a whole new direction and dimension to my mission: like some of my lesser colleagues in inferior uniforms, I can take on a sidekick; we can broaden my mission's scope and m.o. And I can be a father, a mentor to this talented but misguided young man…

"This is an interesting but far-fetched theory, James. I can arrange a meeting with Mayor Hussell, and we can bring it to his attention. If necessary, we can meet with Murd and Attaki on short notice too. They always make room…"

"Give me a break, Supe. You're just a stooge-riding shotgun for these guys. Hussell? He owns 5% of WE. Attaki and Giusillini have half a percent. You think Murd and Mafficante don't deal? Shit, Supe, where've you been? How do you think projects get built in Manhattan? Why do you think Manhattan's low-crime while the boroughs are hellholes ruled by the wiseguys. Shit, you're flying around picking up petty-crime assholes too dumb to know Manhattan is off limits for larceny and violence, and all you're doing is stooging for Sal. You're a one-man royal army, a fuckin' police state, like fuckin' Guatemala."

It's all red again. My head is throbbing, splitting, ringing. I grab James, and I'm going to smash him and his nefarious equipment, but he lets off a blast with an airhorn into my ear, and I fall to the dirty floor.

James hands me a Coke—I feel too weak to resist its unhealthful stimulus.

"I knew this would be tough on you, Supe, so I was prepared."

I'm silent, waiting for the tonic effect of the sugar and caffeine. The noise echoes like a tornado, like the crashing roaring I heard from the cellar at home when we rode out a storm, holding hands and praying. I see a faint figure, perhaps an optical floater—is it Daniel Velt?

James sits down by me. He hands me another Coke.

"Look, Supe, I've been there too. Everything turns to shit, man. You won't believe me, but I'm telling you what Rick has planned. He can't hit Lois, so he and Cherry are going kick her upstairs somewhere and find her a man—lots of men. They're setting her up with both stars of "Starved into Happiness." Want to hear a tape of the muscle-bound Foreman calling her, how excited she is? The guy's a homo, but they know she'll like that. They'll cream over New Age issue shit. Then they've got a whole lineup of straight celebrities to keep her busy—and these guys don't know they're carrying chips that'll pick up everything they do in private. That'll neutralize Lane.

"Duckey'll be castrated in a Betty Ford Southern Comfort clinic; he'll live to make millions on his story of returning from the edge of death in the hands of booze and serial sex. Blarhe's going to lose his voice mysteriously; he'll create a new feel-good Origami poetry and tour as the male Helen Keller, smiling and goo-gooing. I'm buying their stock; they're going to be big, big."

I stand up. I've never been beaten, humiliated like this—to be brought down by a cynical, punk kid! But I know I must go on, even if I don't know what to do.

"JR, you talk tough and cynical, but you and I know there's a good heart inside you, and I'm going to help you find your inner good self. For a long time I've had my eye out for a sidekick, a partner, and you might just fill the bill. You'll become a hero; with some recovery work you can harness that genius to do good."

"Yeah, yeah. But what're you gonna do when Kent's ass gets fired? You're wasting your time with that loser-girl in BedStuy when you should be checking the Hussells' moves. You'd better get out to Long Island and see for yourself."

No one (except Lois of course) tells me what to do. Nobody but lawbreakers talk rude to me like this kid. I tell him to wait for news from me. He doesn't know it, but he's already my sidekick.

I always loved stray dogs on the farm. They'd snarl and snap at me, but they couldn't hurt me. I'd overpower them with affection and food. Sometimes Ezra got jealous, but I'd save special scraps for him, and I'd let him sleep with me, for he was my best friend.

9 BIG BUSINESS BY THE YACHT

"Numbnuts! Asswipe! Shitface! —How did I, Herbert Horatio Hussell, raise a total fuckup?"

"But Dad..."

"Shutup you midget moron. Move away, I'm pissing."

"Good idea, Dad, maybe you'll calm down, I'm trying to tell..."

"Mmm, oohh, mmm. Aaah. Great! Now listen shitface: do you want to spend the rest of your life cleaning honeypots in Bed Stuy? How do you think you're going to get out of this with your little skinny ass?"

"Dad, you don't understand..."

"Oh, yes I do, jerkoff."

"No, no, sorry. What I mean is, I was exploring a new frontier for resources, paradoxically..."

"SHUT UP. Take your goddamn paradigm shaft and shove it up your skinny ass."

I'm hovering in cloud cover I spread at 400 ft. above "Ye Power O' Erin." The Hussells conduct one of their famous media-free sessions, while Mama Hussell cooks for what she knows will be two hungry boys when they climb aboard. Rarely seen in public, she consents to be photographed only at home, and her favorite shot shows her serving Herb a generous dollop of "Hearty Hussell Haggis." Their home on Smithtown Bay is vast, but unpretentious, a colonial ranch with four extensions. Serendipitously, five of their waterfront neighbors sold out within months of their settling in.

"Listen, asshole, I don't know why I have to teach you this shit. Do you think Tweed, Daley, Moses, Murd, and I built our things by blabbing how we do business? You stupid shit, do you think every time Von Umph puts up a super new building ahead of schedule, he tells the world, 'I owe it all to my wiseguy backers?'"

"Yes but he used the media; he's one of my mentors. I visit him at Mar a Phago..."

"Then why didn't you learn something, you little cunt. Sure, the guy's a genius at selling crap at a premium. We bought him because we can make money on him. Idiot hick suckers come to New York to see his fucking doorman, like those stiffs by the Royal Palace in London. Fifty-sixty times I've done business with him. But listen, asshole, tell me when he told the world how the wiseguys paved the way for him with the unions and the city and the truckers. Did he tell the world he owed the *Art of the Come* to CIA Asian drug guys with billions to lay off? Sure he plays the media; he plays them like a hooker's snatch.

"But you. You think your pencil-dick will grow because you hang out with Duckey and Blahre—fine, they're our properties. You got some ideas about manufacturing our art products cheap and making us look like fucking recyclers—do it. But don't hang your fucking silk underwear out for the world to see!

"My New New York, the biggest goddamn market that ever happened: do you think I got the boroughs to stay back and support my Manhattan moves by telling the world how I aligned the outer police and fire precincts with the wise guy crews? Do you think that I tell some asshole jock trader he gets his cigars and his coke and his authentic fucking native art he shows off in his Von Umph limited edition condo because my friends in Miami work with Havana and Bogota cartels?

"You little shit, it's taken me 40 years to build this thing, to get what we have. Nobody, not Tweed, not Joe Kennedy got it lined up around the world like Rupert and me. Rupert can go to Tibet and tell the whole fucking country what he wants. You should see the Dalai Lama nodding and bowing when Rupert comes over on a fucking pilgrimage with five faggot Buddhist movie stars..."

"Dad, some of the pilgrims were heterosexual..."

"Listen, dickhead, you'd better stop trying to explain first-grade shit to me. Are you getting laid?"

"Pardon me?"

"Are you getting laid enough?"

Rick blushed, and so did I. For a fleeting moment I pitied him. I believe I now have insight into his character. His curriculum vitae is a study in the breadth and depth a privileged background can afford. After prep school and little ivy college, he received his Masters in Creative Economic Dynamics from the Streisand New School for Psycho-Social Research, publishing his thesis, "New Trends in the Synchronicity and Synchronitization of Content," in WE's McGraw Barron's *Quick Hits for Rising Execs* CD Rom Series in 2003. His ongoing dialogues with the Dalai Lama, Hillary Clinton and Tom Cruz on "The Wealth of the Angels" are proven fund-raisers for public television.

His appearance rarely heads catalogues of his assets. His jaw, felicitously dubbed "provocatively simian" in the *Inner Vogue* cover story, has caused his media consultants to investigate corrective surgery. Is his image too "hot" for the New Age, they wonder. But they are heartened by the increasing lionization of Kissinger and pro wrestlers, and hope he can ride the trend to images of more-raw masculinity. For Rick belies his diminutive stature with what Norman Mailer, author of the *Inner Vogue* piece calls, "a surging, bouncing big-cat energy to his walk."

Before now, the only contretemps in Rick's career involved minor matters of transportation: lost for hours in his BMW limo in Brooklyn just after the upgraded Bridge reopened, he resolved to waste no more of his precious time. He ordered up a corporate helicopter to fly him about Manhattan and the proximate neighborhoods of the boroughs. He kept a corporate jet ready to fly him to the suburbs and the Hamptons. Landing helicopters all over Manhattan proved impractical, causing evacuations of large and small buildings. His buzzing of Northport and Stony Brook, looking for malls that could land a stretch 737, caused traffic accidents and tie-ups in those townships—but WE assured citizens on the early-evening media that they were being invaded by neither the UN nor any other alien jurisdiction.

Struggling to please his demanding dad, I can now see, is the key to Rick's character. His achievement of independent wealth through canny investments in a sprightly portfolio of REITs and media IPOs—even this crowning achievement failed to satisfy his Dad, whose holdings are comfortably into the eleven figures, while his son struggles to emerge from nine. His alliance as County Leader with Senator T'Omato in streamlining the development of the Island was set up by his Dad: the Senator's and Rick's contributors crisscrossed the Island with new highways connecting to malls and gated upscale townhouse developments.

"Dad, I am more than meeting my needs. I am expressing my sensual self in a healthy variety of ways. In fact…"

"In fact I don't want to hear about it. A young man does stupid shit when he can't get laid. You're getting laid. You're just stupid.

"Do you know where you stand, you little pimple? Do you know that Sal wants you dead and Rupert is o.k. with that? We can arrange a dramatic accident and a media funeral that will make your little ass look gold forever and set up things in your memory that will mean real income to us. You're worth more dead, kid—look at the Kennedys…

"They'll hold off hitting you for a while out of respect for me…"

"Please, Dad, you know I'm bottom-line-oriented."

"No, I want to kick myself for being too stupid to see what a fuckup you are. I should have listened to your Mom: she wanted you to do charity work with your Ivy League buddies. She told me, 'Poor little Rickie is hyperactive.' I should've listened. I thought your spewing this New Age hype would help us with the whacko new cyber-consumers.

"Yeah, I kick myself: I thought you'd see how things work by being out there on the job. But no, you're like a cop who gets too greedy or a dealer hooked on the shit. You're as dumb as Superman. The asshole thinks he's on a fucking noble mission, just like you."

"Dad, let me start over and work my way up."

"Nah, you're out. I've just gotta figure out what to do…"

"Dad, listen…"

"No you listen, you little turd. You're always opening your fat yap. You think I'm ignorant and you've got to bring me up to speed. Look, I did Yale. I was Cross Boners. I studied history. I played football, made the contacts; I learned the game. But you, you took all this New Post PC crap seriously; you wondering whether sheep-shagging is valid fucking sexual discourse. You got hooked.

"Look at Cherry. Sure she reads books. Sure she knows lots of faggots and artists. But she knows the ones that count like Zauberberg. The guy's a genius. He turns the fucking Holocaust into an empire. He makes people feel there's that little ray of hope at the end of the Nazi tunnel because some guys who screws around and has got money saves a few grateful cute ethnic mamas and papas in color outside the Old City. I love it.

"So we buy the Old City, neutralize it from the fucking Jewish and Arab bullshit to make it safe, throw in some rides in the wasted space in front of the Wailing Wall, and now everyone gets off the tour busses at the 'Zauberberg Monument' outside. That plaque gets more attendance than the Stations of the Cross. Tourists stay there to watch WE films about the Promised Land and go to the shops instead of going inside.

"Steve did that. That's Cherry's kind of artist. That's Hollywood. That's Disney. That takes brains.

"—As for you, go do some aquatic aerobic reps, or whatever you call them. I've got to take a shit..."

And while Rick dutifully carves stylish figures in the water, his father continues his lifelong battle with constipation, grunting, cursing and red in the face. I see his flaccid body, its folds multiplied and magnified by the gray-brown waters, pulsing and straining as if it were a large snake trying to disgorge, and I marvel once again at what sorry physiques of men of power and captains of industry. Finally he achieves two large compact results, which float West towards the City.

I feel sick. I struggle to maintain altitude flying home.

I dream that I am a little boy looking just like me. I'm four feet tall in my uniform. JR towers over me, drooling Baby Ruth from the corners of his mouth, his breath sweet and hot. "You're shit, Supe. You're a little turd, a little knobby candyass."

He grabs my right bicep in a grip that dissolves me to scratchy dust, every part of me unable to bear every other part, and I am shrinking in his grip, while Dan Velt laughs in the background, his barking laugh, and unbuckles his pants. "I gonna beat the crap out of that slimy little eschaton." The huge belt-buckle flashes and blinds me. I deflate in JR's grip to my suit, limp, empty. I cannot breathe; sickening hot Baby Ruth blows up my nostrils, envelops me like chloroform.

I wake, limp, wet, scared. But I'm angry and beginning to know where I'm going.

10 DEATH

I always keep my promises, which can require iron discipline. I promised Tyesha that I would visit her; I cannot honestly say that traveling to a slum in a black neighborhood in Brooklyn is a duty that attracts me. This little girl is so hopeless, so removed from the pep and fun I see in normal kids, her parents so sullen and uncaring. James tells me to ditch her. But I cannot in good conscience; I must fly to Brooklyn, even though I know it is unlikely to supply me the emotional uplift to do what I am now driven to.

They live on Nostrand Avenue, over a bodega boarded up when the Magic Center opened. The door to the walkup is smashed, its frame in splinters—probably kicked in during a police raid. I hate to touch this ruin on hinges—it's an encrusted brown; I analyze the crust as pollutants congealed in blood saliva, alcohol, vomit, urine and perspiration painted over twice. Bullet-holes holes cry out for putty. The hall smells of urine, feces, garbage; I retch climbing the stairs that appear to be detaching from their support-wall, along the hall past encrusted doors. What does a child feel going to school or out to play over these once-white patterned tiles coated yellow, red, brown?

The door is ajar. I hear a rasping, grinding sound. It is Tyesha's father, he's talking nonstop, sitting in the hall, hunched over, head bobbing towards his knees. He's alone. His voice grinds into my skull.

"I told her and told her to eat. Shit, I told her. I loved that little girl, even if she wasn't grateful me and her big sister took her in. I loved her. You can't tell me I didn't love her. I loved her. Me and her sis, we loved her. We looked out for her. You can't tell me I didn't love her..."

I find the living room: an old television with 4 little children staring at it in their underwear. Tyesha's mother standing over them, staring at it. There is one sprung couch. Tyesha's mother begins talking as soon as she sees me.

"What she want to go and die for after all we done. She was a bad girl. What she want to go and die for—I fed her, mothered her after her own damn mother overdosed, I've got 4 of my own without that nasty pissy little sister to take care of, what she want to die for. It makes me look bad, shit."

A cab driver lives alone next door. He is standing in his doorway when I leave, and he asks me in. People like to tell me their life stories: he tells me about his clean, Christian life. He sends back money to his auntie in Haiti. I cut him off politely—I am having difficulty understanding him, and I want to know about Tyesha.

"That so sad, Sir. That so sad—she be better off dead and with the Lord, man. All the time her sister was hurting her; they use those drugs man, that little lady was more money from the welfare. I never take the welfare, man; I am a Christian."

And he shows me his picture of a black Jesus who looks just like the normal Jesus except for his dark skin. The picture hangs next to John F. Kennedy's over his sofa, which doubles as his bed. He has no workstation or television, only an ancient radio with knobs. The place smells of detergent; it's clean but dingy.

"They yell at her and they hurt her. The social services here a couple of times, but they don't help. Those addicts, sir, all they care about is these drugs. Sometimes I give her a good meal, but then they yell at me and beat her. She never talk, sir. All she say is, 'I'm crazy. I'm very bad.' I don't understand. Her folks the crazy ones. She's better off with Jesus, sir. I'm sure glad to meet you. My auntie not going to believe Superman came here to Bedford-Stuyvesant. She going to think I'm crazy on her."

I fly to 110 Livingston Street. I visit the Department of Social Services. Nobody knows much, except that Tyesha's mother, an addict who lived a floor above, died three years ago when Tyesha was five. Her studio apartment was furnished, the reports say, with a double bed and a television, and she died of an overdose on the bed where she and Tyesha lived. The caseworker, alerted by the kindergarten teacher to a little girl's two-day absence, found her on the bed with her mother, who emitted a horrible odor, begging her, "Mommie, Mommie, please wake up."

I visit the crack 23rd "Buddy Boy" police precinct, where the case reports, after decrying the absence of marketable goods or fungible drug stashes in Tyesha's final home, detailed the protruding bones and the scars on her body, concluding they are evidence of abuse and starvation by her foster parents, and suggesting the ADA bring them to justice.

11 ROUNDUP

It's a dog day, one of those September days that makes New Yorkers wonder how they lived through the summer. The airless public schools stifle, garbage and human waste in Emerging areas stinks. The City gasps, sweats, and grasps for quick remedies: cold beer, fans, fire hydrants, fire escapes.

I have resolved to remove all middle-class comforts from my well-kept apartment in Douglaston, and my sheets stick to me when I awake. As I admire my sculpted superhuman body and my chiseled good looks, I know that today is my last day. I cannot, I will not resist the rage that courses through my body. I want to weep, and comfort myself with the cool conditioned air; I shrink from donning my suit. But pure heat of my anger melts my insecurities, and I burst through my picture window, leaving a trail of glass fragments. I laugh at the citizens of Queens to whom I have now revealed my identity. I hover over the entrance to the E line, where primary candidates for something shake hands and make promises. I cry down to the crowds, "It's hot. Hug your tubes! It's going to get hotter!"

During flight out Long Island I leave Lois a message from my microcell, "You were right about everything, but it's worse even than even you know. I love you, Lois. Goodbye forever."

The Hussells are at breakfast when I burst into the compound. Mama Hussell screams as I take Herb under one arm and Rick under the other. I fly them off towards LaGuardia in their silk jammies. Headwinds tear off their silk bottoms, which flutter and float to rest in the outfield at Shea Stadium. Rick attempts a phone call, but I heat his phone with my eyes, happy as his fingers sizzle and he drops his prize toy into the brownish waters. Herb is silent, thinking. Rick opens his mouth, but I stop him, "Shut up, little man. I'm giving you the classiest private charter you'll ever want. Right Dad? You feel like big stuff, Herb?"

We pass over LaGuardia; I weave them in and out of the air-traffic pattern, waving to the pilots, dropping first one Hussell then the other, to grab them just before they hit the tarmac and the roofs of Rikers Island.

We alight on Rikers. I leave them on the hottest roof, and do some fast recon. I release the petty criminals awaiting trial for weeks, months, years--the homeless, the squeegee-men, the child and teen street-pushers and users—telling them all to run for it fast. The smell of good food leads me to the Mafia block: Sal's crew is gorging and taking happy-pills. I confiscate their food and dope. "Bye-bye, bad boys," I croon to them as they grunt, growl and tell me I can't do what I just did.

I go to the deepest recesses of the vast black block: African-American men accused of torture, murder, rape; I move half the block, singling out the biggest and angriest, in with the wiseguys. "Bye, Wiseguys, I guess I can't do this either."

Then I bring the Hussells, trying to hide their nakedness behind their silk shirttails, to the black block, where the inmates pound their doors to get at them, but no problem because, I go "Eenie, Meenie, Mieniee, Moe," and then lock each in with the lucky, prizewinning cellmate.

I croon, "Pack up all my cares and go, blackbird, bye-bye."

When I was little I wanted to sing like Bing Crosby and Perry Como.

I pour aviation fuel into the waters around the island, igniting a ring of fire, and I smash the bus-bridge to the island, dropping an empty Delta Shuttle 727 on it.

Then I pay a business call on the CNN studio in the Times Square. The newspros are unaccustomed to covering the news where they broadcast it, except for the financial markets, but under my lash they muster the requisite throbbing metro backdrop and female Asian reporter, and I uncover to the citizens of the free world the nefarious plots and the network of evil exploiting them, effectively parrying the reporters incredulity by playing the unexpurgated audiotapes I made of the Hussells in the waters of Long Island. I must act quickly now I've tipped my hand.

Attaki, Giussilini, Murd, T'Omato and Von Umph are meeting the press in the Fox and Hound Club atop Von Umph's golden tower in Columbus Circle. Laser pointer in hand, Von Umph is showing his partners scale models of the solid phalanx of world's tallest buildings for which he is breaking ground along the Hudson, starting with the all-private Yankee Stadium at 57th Street and proceeding north to Columbia University through the now-condemned Riverside Park. I crash the party through the picture window, and it's a quick trip with the big five over to the Rikers Island block I've staffed for the rich and famous. I tie them together with strips I tear from their designer clothing. The Hussells' cells are silent. I dole out the power-brokers to the shadowy denizens.

Two of Von Umph's towers loom skeletal by the River, taking advantage of the Hussell-Attaki agreement that real estate entrepreneurs, should they wish to shoulder the risk, can build pending environmental approvals. I warn off the crews idling by the chain-link entrances smoking and smacking their lips at the late female commuters, a lawyer for Sal's Building Trades Union having won a case that re-classified verbal sexual harassment as protected speech, and negotiated guidelines for which parts of a woman's body can be named in such expressions. The men are only too happy to cease these labors. I ascend to the exact elevation towards which my inner Tae Kwan Do guides me, and I plummet and split the concrete slabs from windy top to wet subterranean bottom. The buildings fall neatly into their cavernous pits. The hundreds of new buildings spiking Manhattan skies pull at me, I'm dying to crush them, but I must not harm the innocent.

I remove the Disney figures atop the WE Brooklyn Bridge, pull the wallboard murals with scenes from Disney classics from the arches, retrieve the Allegorical Figure of Brooklyn from before the NRA Experience Project (formerly the Brooklyn Museum), and place this classic, my favorite work of art, smack in the middle of the Adams Street ramp.

Military jets, drones and helicopters now patrol the Metropolis, but it's easy to elude their sensors, and they dare not fire at me when I am near populated areas.

My next mission is to New Jersey, a free-fire zone for the military cannons, and so I plunge into the murky harbor before Lady Liberty and streak underwater upriver to the

Meadowlands. Pine stumps dating from the Renaissance impede my subaquatic navigation, but soon I find the two things I am seeking in the seething chemical muck that was New York's first, most beautiful ecology fecund for farmer, fisher, trapper, miner, artist, and logger. Jimmy Hoffa's body is perfectly preserved in a concrete block beneath the 50-yard line at Giants Stadium, his skin a pearly-gray interior designers would do well to emulate in their marble counter-tops, and I place him out of the sun at the head of the famous bridge table in the Tusch family skybox from which deals are done when action is fast and furious on the field. I leave another VMX for Lois. Hoffa looks serene, as if he's finally found his proper forum.

I dredge up and reassemble Pennsylvania Station on the shoulder of the Lincoln Tunnel approach, amazed motorists rubbernecking at its cracked and seamed Italianate glory.

Working quickly, I bend the pillars on all the tracks leading to the Times Square subway complex, and create barriers and small fires forcing its evacuation, and the evacuation of the immediate Times Square area. I do not know if my tribute to the glory of the Metropolis would hold together after its decades in the swamp, and I do not want its renaissance to harm innocent bystanders.

And now I achieve my masterpiece: under heavy gunfire from Apache helicopters I fly Penn Station across the Hudson, the shrapnel chipping its beautiful surface, so that it resembles a European monument victimized by war as much as an American monument victimized by developers. I lay this piece of New York history to rest in the City's deserted center: let the world ponder it. Let this symbol of four centuries' development assail the tourist and entertainment heart. The center of the metropolis stinks like a sewer. As I leave, the bomb squad stealthily maneuvers towards Penn Station, covered by National Guardsmen in riot gear.

Worn but exultant, I check into the Quality Inn near the Vince Lombardi rest stop off Route 95, disguised as a business road warrior.

12 UP AND AWAY

I dream Tyesha is the star of her own TV show, "Tyesha Tells All," as an inquiring reporter in a business suit, and she interviews the god of the free world, our evening newscaster whose voice carries such utter conviction that my whole soul believes His every syllable, and she asks Him about His personal private divine life, the angelic women He escorts while His wife fights obesity in Darien, and why He abandons His children, surprising our god by exposing to Him, one by one, the lost forgotten children for whom He pays no support, and each time a child appears before the god, it sobs and blesses the god for permitting it to come home to Him, for they had missed Him, and each child's face contorts with emotion as miraculously He bestows upon it its father and mother from television, generations begotten by heartwarming Ozzie and Harriet, and the little ones are so hysterically happy to have the homes the parents and love they've never had, that as one they forgive the god before the commercial break, and during the break a pregnant teenage girl and her stubble-faced boyfriend give an ecstatic testimonial to the lavender abortion clinic franchise they enter hand in hand for a cheap procedure that will have them back on the beach within the hour, all credit cards accepted, and Tyesha is older after the commercial and she wears caked makeup and now she is interviewing weeping parents who miss their lovely children taken early to heaven, and Tyesha recommends in the trained voice of a newscaster, the controlled tones of modulated sympathy, healing books to them so they could feel good about themselves as they snivel over pictures of their little lost loved ones, pushing a WE mike into their unpleasant faces, and moving on to the next set of parents as these could struggle to answer her insistent question, how do you feel.

The snivelers deflate with a sigh as the mike withdraws and the new parents puff up as it approaches, all floating away with their books when the commercial returns, and the teen couple are on the creamy white beach staring dreamily into each others' eyes, her hand on his thigh and his on her bottom as they lick their lips and enter the privacy of their lavender cabana suite in the Atlantis Resort City on the widened renovated and elevated Caribbean Barrier Reef, and their lavender sports utility vehicle, lonely outside, shivers and rocks in a sexual motion, and a generation of tanned normal happy families with scores of bubbly normal happy children emerge from the its tailgate and frolic on the beach that has excited the abortion couple.

And I dream that Tyesha appears on the wildly popular "Whacked Home Videos" and the crowd applauds wildly as her older sister grabs her food away from her at her birthday party and chains her to her wet bed, cheering each blow as her sister pounds her prostrate form, and the wildly popular announcer from Wrestlemania keeps score, and the audience boos when Tyesha rises to cry and cheers when her brother-in-law gropes her writhing body and laughs when she slips, slides, and falls in her own vomit rushing to the bathroom, which is occupied and she jumps up and down holding her crotch, and she piddles and we cheer as her brother sternly punishes her, fastening her to the wall next to the bathroom with his belt and he and her sister put out their cigarettes on her and we chortle as they force her to listen to the raucous amplified noises of themselves and her nieces and nephews in the toilet accompanied by hilarious cartoon music, and then our laughter peaks as she watches brother and sis shoot up, and fall asleep copulating at her feet.

And now she is a color picture on a supermarket tabloid, scars, urine, vomit and tears outsized as if pasted on, and obese couples and splotchy retirees, faces frozen in smiles tightened by botox and enlarged by collagen, stare at her as they chew gum on their way from checkout counters from which they pilfer, not knowing they are charged automatically, to their SUVs and their pickups in the Mall of Freedom. And the announcer, a god of the free world wannabee, calls Tyesha back at our instistence in modulated tones of sympathy to cry, burn, cower, cringe, shake, defecate, scratch, scream and sink into a fetal position in which she dies, and at each act the audience applauds and exclaims ooh, aah *appreciatively, as if watching the poses of a bodybuilder or a cute skater landing a triple axle. But the wildest funny part is a little five-year-old Tyesha shaking her Mommie, dead of an overdose on the bed from which she parented her daughter before the TV, shaking her in the ludicrously mistaken hope her Mommie is sleeping, but we know better and each "Mommie, Mommie, please wake up Mommie," is more of a scream.*

I wake, too exhausted, spent and useless to do anything but click the bedside remote at the tube. I look at the Opera Winbig show but I can't understand why she's so interested in what she's saying about herself so I click and see a fat white girl from Detroit on Sally Fessie assaulted verbally and physically by her mother and her stepmother because of her pimples, her fat and the covert lust they spit at her from her pink Dear Diary and I click and see a little girl from Cleveland denounced by her six older brothers and sisters as a bedwetter, her parents waiting seriously and dutifully in the wing with her sheets and nightie to trap her when she denies it, and I click and I see an ad for non-steroidal ginseng-up-down gingko baloba wort tuning in, turning on and toning your brain and spirit and I click and a bible-brandishing lank-haired woman in a tie-died smock denounces her muscular, shaven-headed husband for cheating on her while she took care of seven kids all of them his and I click to a news flash about ethnic and religious cleansing spilling over from Guatemala into Belize the U.S. military the CIA and Benito Banana angrily denying connection and questioning their accusers' loyalty and Borebush and Blair and Fujimori denouncing Fidel and Cesar and Sodom and vowing to bomb and degrade them surgically while on the next channel children with stooped backs and distended bellies allow flies to walk into their eyes and mouths and then the commercial break for a Jersey senatorial candidate running against pregnant teenage welfare cheats—and I know I cannot go on, I can never awake from this nightmare.

So I grab James, and I fly the polluted air and water and dirt of New York for the polluted land of Kansas.

AFTERWORD: METROPOLIS

Superman's problems might be the same as those of Ronald McDonald, if the latter were animated and had problems. Still, he stands out front, totally neuter and without surface suggestive of underlayers, as spokesman for the "6 Billion Sold," then after a while (facing such excess?), just "Billions and Billions." But Superman has surfaces. There's Clark, and under that his unform and under that a girdle of modesty padding (provided by a caring mother?, and under that? He's never had an erection, so when Lois says, "Clark, how do you feel about oral sex?" she might be offering heself as receiving, a kind of communion, even given the long salamis hanging above them at the time. The salamis are commodities, and in this novel qualities of product are never the issue, but only the selling and devouring of them (as with McDonald's burgers? As with erections?).

This is his autobiography, an intention to display the surface, then get under it in order to understand. The self? He has his X-ray vision: "I can see the conical bags of silicone in those breasts, the little clamps on her ovaries." He sees but another surface, one that diffuses any possibility of desire, her body as display of something private, a way to "suppress my imagination, thinking normally, so that I could function as an American." It is exactly that, imagination, that he lacks.

Autobiography begins in narcissism: "I take a private, quiet satisfaction in myself and my feats that is far more potent than the pleasures my fellow-beings get from their sex-acts. I know this for sure; often my work entails surveiling them doing sex. I am proud to say that I have never had an erection." The voyeur is a narcissist, observing himself as observer, and though seeing, even through X-ray vision, sees not much of the others, but for surfaces under the surface, nothing at all that will result in connection. Even near the end, where Supe rises into the sky holding the poor child Tyesha, he's victim of the splendor of his cape and clothing, only vaguely curious about her destitution.

Yet autobiography might end in knowledge, if not of the self, at least in discoveries about the self's place in the world, in this case the discovery that he is not more than a shill for Rupert Murd's World Enterprises Plc, WE, that world wide commercial engine making a commodity of everything, including himself.

WE, MCFE, MAMA, the book is full such acronyms, and they, together with an ongoing tortured business lingo, create an Orwellian world, though one burlesqued in roman a clef, most notably in the characters of two poets, Robert Duckey and James Blahre. Recent personages appear, hardly veiled, and time is torqued through a conflation of past and present. Michael Jordan has died, for example, 2000 seems far in the future at times, or in the past. Dreams may regularize: Supesees himself "disappear into the [computer] screen, into red dots that sear my skin, and I shatter into glass fragments scraping themselves," some early image of his place only as a manipulated icon.

I think of three versions of metropolis. There's New York City of course (the place in this novel), a real place, but Gotham City too, so named, satirically, by Washington Irving in Salmagundi Papers, a place to wake up in, disoriented and off center. Then there's the great Metropolis of Fritz Lang, that 1926 movie (set, curiously, in 2000) in which the Art Deco city scape is the central character, a twisted utopia, the people in it strangle disconnected, in dress and attitude, from the physical world they find themselves within. There's the saintly Maria, then the Frankenstein like creation of the vil one, the revolutionary. The double, of course, and perhaps autobiography can move below surface, that narcissism, and discover the true self. Supe certainly becomes the revolutionary here, rearranging the city in which he'd been held in bondage, though this rearrangement seems enraged and excessive, almost adolescent. What exactly has he discovered, about the self under that costume?

And the last one, Metropolis, Rintaro's tour de force of Japanese anime in which human figures are cartoon like, though set against a magnificent and infinitely complex city so real that it seems unreal. In My Last Days the city is animated by language, no less halluninatory. It's a machine, the people are cogs, and only one might fly, up, up and away, in search of self knowledge and freedom.

—Toby Olson

IN MEMORY

Vanessa Green
Barbara Reisley

Printed in the United States
123160LV00001B/181-213/A

9 780978 549961